WITCH IN A WOLF DEN

HANKS HOLLOW SERIES BOOK TWO

RACHELLE KAMPEN

ONE

ROSIE

LYING ON THE HARD GROUND, WITH HER HAIR tangled among the pine needles, sticks, and debris, Rosie Hart was sure she was in heaven. She stretched her neck and stared up at the bright clouds that puffed along the blue expanse of sky.

"What about that one?" she asked, pointing at a cloud that looked like a rabbit.

Lucas's head rested on her stomach, his hair splayed out in a halo of brown tufts over her white T-shirt. She combed her fingers through the soft locks as he squinted, trying to pick out a picture among the fluffy white marshmallows in the sky.

"Bunny?" he asked.

"Yep." Rosie grinned. "I totally see a bunny."

The warm pressure of Lucas's head disappeared as he sat up, and Rosie's grin faded at the sudden loss of contact. He turned and lay on his side, propping his head up with his arm. His T-shirt rode up, exposing his skin, and Rosie reached out to tickle him. He caught her hand and laughed. A smile lingered on his face as he held on, then it dropped into a frown. "We have to get back. It's time."

"Already?" Rosie squeezed her eyes shut and took

a deep breath through her nose. "I don't want to go back."

Going back to the house meant no more touching. No more kissing. No outward displays of affection. They'd gotten good at keeping their relationship a secret. Summer had passed, and no one had caught on.

"I'm sorry, Rosie." Lucas pressed a soft kiss to her lips as his hand skimmed her arm, leaving a tingly trail of electricity over her skin. "I don't want to, either, but we've been out here for two hours. Your grandma is expecting you, and my dad will be looking for me soon."

"Just a little longer?"

His mouth opened, and she thought he was going to argue. Something in his sea-blue eyes shifted as he stared into her face. Instead of speaking, he captured her mouth in his. She returned the kiss, running her fingers through his mop of thick hair.

The primal drive took over as her desire deepened. The flames of the mate bond roared to life, and she curled her body into his. In response, he moved on top of her, trailed his hand down her side and to her hip, and pulled her closer. Heat and desire built with each soft kiss, intensifying to a level that scared and excited her, to the point that her wild wolf urges almost became uncontrollable. With a low, regretful moan, Lucas broke away, and Rosie sighed.

As she came down from the high of their kiss, her cheeks heated. Good thing Lucas had more control over his wolf urges than she had over hers. The human side of her wasn't ready to take the next step, and he knew that. Plus, their love was sort of forbidden.

Rosie was the only female werewolf in existence. Normally, werewolf children were males. Her father had secretly fallen in love with a witch, and Rosie was the product of that love. Half witch. Half werewolf.

The United States Werewolf Council had deliberated with the World Werewolf Council over what to do with her. Many wanted her to die, insisting that females had no place in the werewolf world. Her father hadn't told them she was half witch. If he had, her fate might have been sealed immediately. Rosie cringed knowing so many werewolves actually wanted her dead. In the end, those who believed her existence was the will of the gods—a gift given to them to replace the witches who'd abandoned them—had overruled those old-fashioned, misogynistic werewolves who believed she was an abomination.

Not all werewolves still believed in the old stories of the Chosen—the original werewolves and witches created by the gods to protect humans. The Chosen had lived in harmony and worked together. When witch hunts started, the female Chosen—the witches —went into hiding. Without the witches, the male Chosen—werewolves—were left to find a way to grow their packs while keeping their existence a secret...or face extinction.

Though she was glad the Council had decided to let her live, her life wasn't her own. They had plans for her. The order was clear. She had to mate with an alpha.

And Lucas wasn't an alpha. At least not yet.

"You're going to see the Becketts today?" Rosie studied Lucas's face.

His soft hair fell over his dark eyebrows as he nodded. "Yeah. My training is coming along really well. Shawn is teaching me a lot."

"Are you sure you want to be alpha?"

He stared into her eyes with such intensity that it

made her breath seize in her lungs. "I told you. I'll do anything to be with you. If the Council wants an alpha, I'll be an alpha."

Lucas Beckett and his father, Roger, were the only members of the Hart pack who weren't part of the Hart family. Only a member of the family bloodline could become alpha. The role of future leader of the Hart pack was going to Rosie's brother, Sam. Rosie's father, the current alpha, did his best to prepare a reluctant Sam to take over.

Roger and Lucas had joined the Hart pack when Lucas was six, after Roger challenged the Beckett pack alpha, Marcus Beckett, and lost. Months ago, after the Council ordered that Rosie mate with an alpha, Lucas shared with Rosie that he and his father had been meeting with the other Beckett pack members in secret ever since they'd been banished ten years ago. He'd made a promise to Rosie. He would become alpha of the Beckett pack one day.

At only sixteen years old, she hoped she had a few years before she needed to worry about the Council forcing her hand, but she prayed Lucas would fulfill his promise before her fate was decided.

A sudden vibration tickled Rosie's hip, eliciting a giggle.

Lucas rolled off her with a shy smile then fished his phone out of his pocket. "It's my dad. He says it's time to go."

Dirt and dead pine needles littered the back of Lucas's old Misfits T-shirt and faded jeans as he stood. He turned toward Rosie, letting his eyes drift over her before extending his hand. Rosie laced her fingers through his, and he pulled her up to her feet. Over the summer, he'd grown at least three inches. The top of her head barely reached his shoulder.

When she rested against him, her ear pressed over his heart, and the soft beat soothed her.

A low chuckle rumbled in Lucas's chest.

"What's so funny?" Rosie looked up into his amused gaze.

"You have sticks in your hair."

Rosie ducked her head bashfully, and her hand flew to her head. As she finger-combed her curls, she plucked out a twig. She smiled as Lucas helped her get out the rest of the debris.

"I think we got it all," Lucas said as he inspected her tangled curls.

Puffing his cheeks, he blew a long, slow breath out through his mouth as he trained his brilliant blue eyes on her. She slipped her fingers into his outstretched hand, and they stepped through the trees toward the house. When they neared the edge of the forest, Rosie reluctantly dropped Lucas's hand before they reached the sprawling, open yard behind Hart House.

She patted her oak tree as they passed it, and she felt the answering vibration of life from her old friend as the branches rustled, the leaves softly brushing her cheek in greeting.

Silently, they crossed the lawn. Blades of grass swished against Rosie's bare feet. They entered the house through the back patio door, which led to the formal dining room, where her father sat at the head of the twelve-person table. He looked more formidable than usual, with a coffee cup in one hand and his tablet in the other. Probably reading through the local news as he did most mornings.

When he glanced up as they entered, his eyes narrowed. "Good morning, Rosie, Lucas. Did you enjoy your hike?"

They'd been going for "hikes" every morning

since the start of the summer. As far as anyone in the pack house knew, they were just out walking together, nothing more. Rosie's father couldn't find out about their relationship. As alpha, he had a duty to uphold the Council's wishes in his pack.

Rosie was pretty sure Sam knew something was going on between them, but so far, he hadn't said a word. He'd joined them on a few of their hikes, and the awkward silence spoke volumes. Her brother wasn't stupid.

"It was great. Thanks, Dad." Rosie gave her father a kiss on the cheek before she sat down next to him.

Behind her, Lucas cleared his throat. "Yes, sir. It was a great morning for it."

"Too bad you kids won't be able to get your daily exercise once school starts next week."

"Ugh. Don't remind me." Rosie dreaded the start of the school year. Not just because summer would be over but also because she would be forced to face the ugly rumors flying around about her. The rumors that she'd thrown herself at Mason Lewis.

It was bad enough she'd been labeled a freak her entire life. Now she had the label of slutty freak. Her best friend, Becca Miller, had done a lot of damage control. Unlike Rosie, Becca was a social butterfly. Everyone's friend. She'd all but screamed from the rooftops that Mason was a lying jerk.

The truth was that Mason had tried to force himself on Rosie, and she hated thinking about what might have happened if Lucas hadn't shown up and broken Mason's nose before it went too far. Rosie shivered as the memories from that night came crashing down on her. What almost happened. And what she learned. She'd been fooled into thinking Mason shared her interest in wildlife. In truth, he was a killer. His interest had nothing to do with a love of animals and nature and everything to do with seeing what he could stuff and mount on a wall.

Rosie had nothing against hunting in general. As a werewolf, she'd done her fair share of killing. But Mason and his father didn't hunt for the purpose of conservation, population control, or food. Their trophy room was full of mounted deer heads and pelts laid out on display. When Rosie had laid eyes on the wolf stuffed and mounted to a pedestal, she nearly lost her lunch. Even worse was listening to the way Mason described the thrill of the hunt, like he was aroused by it. The memory left her stomach roiling even now.

"Hey." Lucas touched her elbow. "I have to go. My father is waiting. You good?"

Shaking off her thoughts and trying to mask her hurt and fear, she smiled. "I'm good. Have a fun afternoon with Roger."

Another secret to be kept from Rosie's father. He couldn't know about Roger and Lucas's monthly meetings with the Beckett pack. Not when they were hiding it from Marcus Beckett. It would be asking too much of Simon to withhold that kind of information from another alpha. Instead, each month when Roger and Lucas took a day off to meet with the Beckett pack, they told Simon they were out for some father-son bonding time.

As Lucas left, Rosie turned to her father. A tiny trace of crow's-feet formed around his eyes as he scowled at his tablet. His tanned features, honey-brown hair, and large, muscular build had all the ladies in the PTA swooning.

"I need to go too. Grandma is waiting." Over the summer, Rosie had been trying to visit her grandmother at least once a week. The time had paid off. Her magic strengthened every day, and Clara helped her control it.

"I've been meaning to talk to you about that." Simon cleared his throat. "Sam has been complaining about you taking the SUV every week to go see your grandma."

"What? Dad, I can't ask Grandma to come and pick me up here. That's not fair—"

"Ah, Rosie, stop. I'm not going to make your grandma drive here to get you."

Rosie scrunched her face up in confusion. "Then what are you saying?"

Simon sighed. "I'm saying we need to get you your own car."

"What?" Rosie squealed. "Are you serious?"

"Yeah." Her father scowled, and she could feel his irritation as she jumped out of her chair and threw her arms around him. Simon hated flaunting their money. "But you aren't getting a new one. Michael already has the truck for hauling supplies for the rentals, so he really doesn't need his Jeep too. He's going to give it a tune-up first. It will be ready for you by the time you start school on Monday."

Rosie's cousin, Michael, took care of all the vehicles owned by the pack. The Wrangler was his favorite, and he took good care of it. It didn't matter what kind of car it was, though. The idea of not having to argue with Sam about who got to use their shared Ford Explorer had her on cloud nine. "Did Sam say he needs the SUV today? If so, I can ask Roger and Lucas if they'll drop me off at Grandma's."

"Sam won't be needing a vehicle today. I need him here."

"Hm." Rosie pursed her lips. "Pack business?"

Simon nodded. "William and Calvin Cramer are stopping by."

Her eyes widened. William Cramer was alpha to the neighboring Cramer pack. Calvin was his son. Packs didn't just drop in on one another.

Opening herself up to her father's energy, she felt his worry pour over her. She reached out hesitantly, wanting to calm him with the touch of her fingers, but she pulled her hand back. Her father tended to like to stew in his emotions. She'd never tried to use her calming touch on him. "What do they want?"

"I don't know. But don't worry about it. I'm sure it's nothing."

"Well, now I'm really glad I'm going to Grandma's." Rosie shuddered as she thought about the Cramers' last visit. "No offense, but you couldn't pay me enough to be here today."

HALF AN HOUR LATER, Rosie pulled into the driveway of her grandmother's little cottage on the outskirts of Hanks Hollow. Summer annuals blossomed in an array of colors in baskets along the porch and in carefully placed displays planted in the ground on either side of the gated walkway leading to the front steps. Their fragrance mingled with pine from the forest. When the breeze picked up on hot, humid summer days, it carried the fishy smell of the lake behind the house.

As expected, Clara was busying herself among the flowers. A bright-red dress with pink plaid stripes flowed over her solid form, and her long gray hair was gathered in a bun under a big sunhat.

"There she is." Clara stopped what she was

doing to give Rosie a hug as she stepped into the garden. "I was beginning to think you weren't coming."

"Of course I came. I told you I'd be here."

Holding her gaze for a moment, Clara narrowed her eyes. "Hm. Glad you could pry yourself away from Lucas long enough to come and visit your grandma."

"W-What?" She tucked a few loose strands of hair behind her ear and bit her lip. "What are you talking about?"

"Don't play coy with me, Rose Hart. You're in love. It pours out of you. You've been in love all summer."

It was useless to lie to her grandmother. "Why haven't you said anything?"

"Why haven't *you* said anything? I'm a little hurt that I had to call you out." Clara went back to watering her begonias. Little red flowers magically bloomed as she ran her fingers over the plants.

"We haven't told anyone. I don't want my dad to know. He could get in trouble with the Council—"

"*Psh.*" Clara flicked her hand. "A bunch of arrogant old assholes who think they can control everyone's lives."

"I have to do what they say, Grandma. If I don't, they might kill me."

Her grandma turned to her. "That's why you need to learn how to protect yourself."

"I don't think making plants grow and healing injuries is going to protect me from bloodthirsty werewolves."

"Not with an attitude like that, it's not." Clara turned back to her flowers. "You're a lot more powerful than you give yourself credit for, Rosie. More powerful than I'll ever be. More powerful than any witch."

Something caught in Rosie's throat. Clara was her compass, her protector, her mentor. For her to suggest that Rosie was more powerful than she was caused fear like no other. "Stop, Grandma. That's not true."

"It is true, child." Clara sat down on the concrete garden bench and patted the seat next to her.

Rosie sighed before she flopped down onto the bench.

"Rosie, I'm so proud of you. You've made so much progress this summer. But I'm afraid you've outgrown me."

"No, Grandma—"

"Hush. Don't interrupt me."

Rosie snapped her mouth shut at Clara's scolding tone.

"I don't have anything more to teach you. Not where your magic is concerned. You can do things I've never seen."

As though illustrating her point, a goldfinch landed on Rosie's knee. Rosie held out her finger, and the bird accepted her invitation, perched for a moment, then jumped into the air and flew away.

"The living things of this world are drawn to you. And I think there is more you can do. I just don't know how to guide you anymore."

Dread settled in Rosie's stomach, and tears stung her eyes. She squeezed them shut and dug her fingernails into her palms. "Grandma, you're scaring me."

"There's no reason to be scared. Your magic is something to be celebrated, dear. It's such a beautiful thing." Clara patted Rosie's knee. Though the words were soothing, Rosie could feel her grandmother's sadness. "Now, if you would like to learn more about how to make some calming oils out of a lavender plant, I can help you with that."

Rosie wiped at her eyes and forced a smile. "I would love to learn that, Grandma."

"Good. Now. I'm hungry. Let's go inside and get some lunch."

Rosie watched as her grandma got up from the bench and moved up the path toward the front porch. As Clara stepped into the house, Rosie's smile dropped, and the fear returned. Her grandmother was the wisest, most powerful person she knew. If Clara couldn't teach her to use her magic, who would?

TWO

SAM

THE CRAMERS ROLLED UP IN THEIR OBNOXIOUS white Escalade, and Sam fought an eye roll as William and Calvin climbed out. William held his smug nose so high that Sam could practically count his nose hairs. Calvin crept behind him like a shadow, nervously avoiding eye contact.

"Simon. Thank you for taking the time to meet with us." William extended his hand.

Simon shook it. "Of course, William. I apologize for the informal reception."

"Don't think on it. This will be short and sweet. I just wanted us to talk. Alpha to alpha." William gestured to Sam and Calvin. "Future alpha to future alpha. Perhaps more frequent, informal visits wouldn't be such a bad idea. The boys can get to know each other. We're neighbors, after all."

Simon nodded as he gestured toward the front door. "Please, come in."

Sam led the way up the stone stairs, across the veranda, and through the front door into the foyer. Once inside, he waited for William and Calvin to follow before leading them into the office. Simon trailed behind, and he nodded toward Sam as he closed the door. They'd practiced this.

Sam gritted his teeth in irritation before he spoke. "Can I get either of you anything? A drink?"

William's mouth twitched up in a smile. "Good boy. Yes, I'll take a bourbon. Calvin will have some water." He turned to Simon. "I've tried getting the boy to like the hard stuff, but all he can stomach is a weak beer every once in a while."

"Please, have a seat." Simon gestured to the leather couch in front of the fireplace before taking a seat in one of the two matching armchairs opposite. "Now. How can I help you?"

Keeping one ear to the conversation, Sam moved to the wet bar and poured bourbon into two glasses for William and Simon, all the while counting down from ten in his head to calm himself. He reached into the mini fridge and took out two small bottles of water for himself and Calvin. He was on his fifth or sixth time counting down, but anger still simmered in his veins. He had promised his father to try to hold his tongue and behave. The pompous ass sitting on the couch made it so damn hard, though. His mind kept replaying the visit last spring and the way William treated Rosie and Martha. The way he spoke as though Rosie were breeding stock and Martha were an old horse to be taken out back and shot. It turned his stomach.

"I won't waste your time with too many pleas-antries. I know how you like to get straight to the point, Simon." William paused and smiled as Sam handed him his drink. "I'd like to arrange a courtship between your daughter and my son. I think the best way to go about doing that is to have her stay at

Cramer House. I would like to bring her into my pack."

In the midst of handing Calvin his water, Sam's fingers lost feeling, and he dropped the bottle onto the coffee table. It landed with a loud clatter, and Calvin hurried to pick it up. He gave Sam a small nod of thanks, and Sam noted Calvin's shaking hands as he fumbled with the cap, twisting it off and taking a sip.

"Such a clumsy kid." William laughed as he patted Calvin on the back. "Can you manage, son?"

Calvin nodded quickly, and no one bothered to call attention to the obvious fact that Sam had dropped the drink. Sam sat in the other armchair, and his gaze went straight to his father. It took every ounce of restraint not to tell William where to stick it.

"A courtship?" Simon chuckled. "Isn't that a little old-fashioned, William?"

"Maybe." William shrugged as he took a sip of his drink and crossed one leg over the other. "But this is a unique situation we find ourselves in."

Simon's brow wrinkled. "How so?"

"You know Roland and I are close. He is my uncle, after all. He was alpha before he joined the Council and handed the reins over to me. We talk. Often." William took a long, slow drink. "He mentioned his visit with you a couple months back."

A muscle tensed in Simon's jaw. "I didn't realize the Council was making this a public affair. That seems a little reckless."

"I don't think they're making it public, Simon. But as I said, we're close."

"I see." Simon took a drink from his own glass. "Well, I certainly didn't get the impression that the Council wants Rosie to pair up with an alpha so soon.

She's only sixteen. I think sending her off to live with another pack is a little extreme."

"Of course." William waved his hand dismissively. "I'm not saying they should mate right away. However, you have to think about this, Simon. If you want Rosie to stay in Wisconsin, of course you'll want her to find a suitor from my pack or the Beckett pack. I'm offering you my son—a much better choice than what you'll get in the Beckett pack. Marcus Beckett is nearly sixty years old, and Shawn, his next in line, is hardly a fit alpha. He's a hippie. Do you really want her to be with a sixty-year-old drunk or a hippie?" William's face puckered like he smelled something awful.

Simon set his glass down, leaned back in his chair, and eyed William. "I think we have a few years before we need to worry about this."

"Of course," William said. "However, don't you think it's best they get to know each other now? It may make things easier when it's time for her to start producing offspring."

"I think this conversation is over." The muscle twitched in Simon's jaw again, and Sam wished his father would punch William's lights out. Clearly, he wanted to.

William didn't move. Instead, he stared into his glass before taking another drink. "Roland and I do talk a lot."

"So you've said."

"And of course, he's part of the Council. The Council who ordered your daughter to mate with an alpha. I would hate for them to get the idea you're ignoring their orders."

Sam leaped to his feet. "You son of a bitch!"

"Sam!" Simon rose and positioned himself between Sam and the Cramers. "Sit. Down."

"Really, Simon." William *tsked* before he took another drink. "You need to get your future alpha under control."

Next to William, Calvin was a statue. He hadn't moved once since he'd sat down. His eyes stayed glued to the water bottle in his lap, where he fidgeted with the cap.

"I appreciate your visit, William." Simon's voice was polite but firm. "I think it's time for you to leave."

William stared at Simon for a moment before his gaze slid to Sam. A smug grin crept across his face, and he stood. "We go way back, Simon. I tried doing this the easy way." He straightened his suit jacket. "That girl of yours is the key to a new future. My son is the most logical mate. We can make this easy for her. Or we can make it hard. Very hard."

Twitching his mouth in another smug smile, William nodded at Simon before he drifted toward the front door. Calvin remained a shadow behind him.

After the front door closed, Simon spun on Sam. "When will you learn, Sam? You promised to behave."

Not sure he'd heard his father right, Sam spluttered. "Are you serious? Did you hear him? How can you let him talk to you like that?"

"Sam, letting your temper get the best of you is the fastest way to lose an argument."

"Whatever. You're not actually going to do this, are you? You're not going to make Rosie have a *courtship* with that amoeba?"

"Of course not, Sam. But we do need to take his threat seriously."

"She's sixteen!"

"I know that! But Calvin is the most logical choice when the Council eventually orders Rosie to follow through with..." Simon's voice drifted off. He couldn't even finish the sentence.

"With what, Dad? *Mating* with him? God, this is sick."

"Don't you think I know that, Sam? Jesus, I don't want this." Simon ran his hand through his hair. Sam had never seen him look so shaken, and he watched silently as his father suddenly stormed out of the room, his shout echoing through the foyer behind him. "Shit!"

THREE

LUCAS

Lucas laid his jack of hearts on top of the ace Travis had confidently slapped down on the table a moment earlier. "Bump!"

A chorus of shouts followed, and Lucas laughed at the crestfallen expression on his cousin's face.

Travis's jaw dropped as he stared at the right bower before he turned his gaze on Lucas. "You little son of a—"

"Hey!" Roger yelled, his rail-thin frame leaning forward in his chair. "I told you the kid likes to lay in the weeds!"

"Damn, kid!" Shawn laughed as he raised a hand up so that Lucas could give him a high-five. "Now that's a partner!"

"Good game, boys," Roger said with a chuckle.

Travis swept his red hair out of his eyes and picked up the cards. He stared at Lucas as he started shuffling. "That's just bull. You've never beaten me before, you little twerp. Your old man has been coaching you, hasn't he?"

With a shrug, Lucas smiled. "Maybe I'm just a natural."

Travis took a long drink from his bottle of ale as

he pointed at Lucas. "You're gonna be my partner next round."

Roger shook his head and touched a hand to his neatly combed hair. "No can do, Travis. We need to head home. It's getting late, and we have a long drive."

"Come on. One more game."

"Trav." Shawn slapped his cousin on the back. "Let it go. So you got beat by a sixteen-year-old punk. Not like the guys at the brewery are going to think any less of you."

"Oh no." Travis turned a deathly glare on Shawn. "You wouldn't—"

"Wouldn't what? Tell everyone that the biggest smack-talking, self-proclaimed euchre genius got beat so they can tease you about it incessantly for the next month? No. Wouldn't dream of it."

"You're a dick."

"Runs in the family, cuz." Shawn smiled as he took a swig of his beer.

Roger chuckled again and slid his chair out as he stood. "Come on, Lucas. Time to hit the road." He swiveled toward the bar where his uncle—Travis's father—talked with the bartender. "Hey, Christopher. We're headed out. It was good to see you."

"Great to see you guys." Christopher waved. "Have a safe trip."

"I'll walk you out," Shawn said as he stood to his full height, dwarfing everyone else in the room. Everything about Shawn was large. Taller than most people, with long limbs, big hands, and enormous feet he constantly tripped over. His shaggy mop of unruly dark hair, old band T-shirt, and faded jeans complemented the carefree vibe that emanated from the peace-loving man. A clumsy pacifist—not your typical pick for alpha.

Roger and Lucas followed Shawn, and they exited through the back door. The sky was starting to darken, and a pole light cast a yellow glow over the parking lot. The sound of their shoes scraping against the gravel stones echoed through the air as they walked to Roger's car.

"You did good today, Lucas." Shawn stuck his hands into his pockets and looked up at the sky as they walked. "And I'm not just talking about the card game."

Lucas stayed silent as he glanced back at The Wild Boar, the small-town bar where they'd met every month for as long as he could remember. Their meetings kept Roger and Lucas in touch with the rest of their family, minus Marcus and his ten-year-old son, Brody. Each month, after discussing pack business with Shawn and Roger, Lucas enjoyed drinks and card games with his family.

Months ago, Shawn had told Lucas he intended to bring Roger and Lucas back into the pack as soon as he became alpha, then he would make Lucas alpha. Brody was Marcus's preferred successor, but the current alpha was old and in failing health. It wasn't likely he would live long enough for Brody to follow him. Shawn was officially next in line, but he loved the craft beer business, not playing wolf politics.

At first, Lucas hadn't had any interest in taking over. That changed when the Council ordered Rosie to mate with an alpha. Lucas wanted nothing more than to be with her. If that meant being alpha, he would do whatever it took.

"You're going to make a good alpha, Lucas," Shawn said. "You've got what it takes to lead this pack."

Never one to take praise gracefully, Lucas ducked his head. "I'll try my best."

"That's all we can ask."

"But what if..." He'd been afraid to ask the uncomfortable question. "What if Marcus is still alive when Brody is old enough to take over? Will Marcus change his choice of succession?"

"It won't come to that," Shawn said. "I can guarantee it. I'm more worried about the present."

Roger stopped walking and looked at his brother. "What do you mean?"

Shawn sighed. "Marcus's drinking is fogging his judgement. He's making dumb decisions. I worry for his kid, actually. They don't stay in the pack house. Marcus built another house by the river for the two of them and Brody's nanny. I think he just wanted to be away from the pack. The nanny's come over to the pack house, complaining about him a few times. He shows up at the brewery drunk. The town meetings too. He even passed out drunk when the Council visited us a couple of months ago. They weren't impressed.

"Even worse, he's been chummy with William Cramer. I always knew Marcus liked the old traditions, but he's never tried to force them on the pack. Keeping company with the Cramers might change that. I pray we still have a few years, but I'm afraid we'll need to find a way to oust him before he dies."

"You mean..." Lucas swallowed. "You mean you plan to challenge him?" He tried to imagine his gentle giant of an uncle fighting Marcus. It wouldn't go well.

"Not me, Lucas." Shawn shook his head. "It needs to be you."

∾

THE HEADLIGHTS of Roger's little sedan barely provided enough light in the moonless night as they drove through the dense forests of northern Wisconsin. Lucas stared out the window at the blackness, his mind replaying the conversation over and over.

"Penny for your thoughts?" Roger's voice cut through the silence. He was never one for driving with the radio on.

"I think you know what I'm thinking about."

"Hey. You've got a few years before you need to worry about that, okay? Like Shawn said, no one expects you to take over before you're eighteen."

"Yeah, I know. But challenging Marcus? That's heavy, Dad."

"I know. Let's hope it won't come to that."

"But what if it does?" Lucas had spent the last several months preparing to be handed the role of alpha and hadn't thought he would have to fight for it. He would do anything for Rosie, but what if he failed?

Roger looked at Lucas for a moment before he turned his gaze back to the road. "You need to be ready, son."

"Ready how?"

"You're in good shape, Lucas. But don't make the same mistake I did. Don't underestimate him. He's strong. You need to be stronger." Roger paused, taking a deep breath. "And you need to really want this. For the good of the pack. Not just to win Rosie."

Lucas's head swiveled to his father. "What?"

"Come on, son. Do you think I didn't notice how your attitude toward being alpha changed the second the Harts got their visit from the Council? And do you really think I don't know that you and Rosie are doing more than hiking every morning when you disappear into the woods?" Roger grinned at Lucas. "Give your old man some credit."

Thank God for the cover of darkness. From the heat flooding his cheeks, Lucas figured his face had turned beet red. "Are you mad?"

"No. You've been in love with that girl for years." Roger chuckled as Lucas stared at him. "Lucas, I'm your father. I know things. But you need to do what's best for the pack. That's the first duty of an alpha. To always do what's best for the pack."

"I understand." Lucas looked back out the window. He wasn't ready to tell his father what he wanted to hear. He would work hard for the pack. And he would try his hardest to do what was right. But he would never put the pack ahead of Rosie.

FOUR

ROSIE

Rosie was still reeling from her visit with her grandma when she returned to Hart House. As she stepped through the door, she winced. The tension in the air was so thick that it was like hitting a wall. She turned her head to the left, toward her father's office. The pocket doors were slightly ajar, and raised voices signaled an argument.

Not wanting any part of that, Rosie strolled toward the stairs. As she took the first step, she froze when she heard her name. They were talking about *her*. She swiveled toward the office and peeked through the doors.

The entire pack was congregated in the office. Her father stood by the fireplace, his shoulders tense, his hand leaning against the mantel. Daniel and Stuart sat on the leather couch, and across from them, Roger and Michael sat in the matching armchairs. Amos stood off to the side, a scowl on his face, his arms crossed tightly over his chest. Sam sat in Simon's office chair, swiveling back and forth like an antsy eight-year-old.

Lucas stood behind Sam, leaning against the windowsill of the large bay window that overlooked the backyard. His nails dug into the framework, and his face was pinched with so much tension that Rosie fought the urge to run to him.

"Was there a pack meeting tonight?" Rosie spoke quietly, but her voice captured everyone's attention, and the tension in the room elevated even more. "Why wasn't I invited?"

She wanted to laugh...to make light of being left out or forgotten. But the heaviness of their stares only made her frown.

"Rosie, take a seat." Simon gestured toward the chair next to his desk, across from Sam. "We need to talk."

"Okay." Rosie's eyes darted toward Lucas as she walked to the chair. Silently, she asked him for help.

His brow furrowed, and his face scrunched like he was in pain. He bit his lip then looked away.

After Rosie slid into the chair, Simon moved in front of her. He stood close, and Rosie had to raise her head to look into his face.

He cleared his throat. "William Cramer has requested that you start courting his son, Calvin. He wants to bring you into his pack."

Without thinking, Rosie snapped her gaze to Lucas. He wouldn't meet her eyes. Cold loneliness cut through her insides like a knife and left a gaping hole. Her eyes drifted around the room, to the faces of her family—her pack. They all stared at her. Their sadness hit her hard. Loss. Like they'd already accepted she would be leaving them.

The loneliness grew, and tears burned her eyes. Her fate had been decided. She would be sent off to live with strangers, with monsters. She had no say in this? How could they have this meeting without her? Anger crept out of the gaping hole inside like tiny spiders. It tickled over her, moving up her skin. It started in her fingertips and worked its way up through her arms, to her shoulders then the top of her head. When her eyes landed on her father, she narrowed them.

"And you thought you would gather all the boys to decide my fate then hand it down to me like a sentence? You didn't think it was important to include *me* in this conversation?" She raised her voice and stabbed at her chest as the anger bubbled over. "How dare you!"

"Rose!" Simon's face reddened, and his shout bounced off the walls. He opened his mouth to speak again, but he paused. His eyes met Rosie's, and something in them shifted. The anger melted away, and Rosie saw a flash of fear and hurt. Her father's emotions always played in his eyes like a symphony.

"No one wants this, Rosie." Sam's voice was low. "We won't let it happen."

Simon closed his eyes and sighed.

"Right, Dad?" Sam asked.

Rosie already knew. His helplessness and fear came off him in waves. It scared her. Just like her grandmother, her father had always been a solid, strong presence in her life. The emotions she felt from him now were foreign and strange and terrifying.

"We may not have a choice," Simon said. "William threatened to go to the Council. It may be just a matter of time."

And just like that, in one day, the shoulders of the two strongest people in her life—her grandma and her father—which she'd stood on from day one, buckled and broke underneath her.

~

Rosie's breathing came in harsh pants as she stomped across the yard toward the trees. Behind her, Lucas jogged to keep up. Her short, angry strides were no match for his long legs, but she had a head start. She'd left her father's office in a hurry.

"Rosie, wait," he pleaded.

"Go away, Lucas." Inside, the flames of her mate bond roared angrily. The usual steady warmth was replaced with scorching heat. The flame of the bond was a living, breathing thing. It burned warm and pleasant when she was near Lucas and diminished and left her cold when she wasn't. Now, this anger she felt for him seemed to anger the flames of the bond, which licked at her, burning, scolding.

She reached her tree and immediately reached out to the trunk, seeking its strength and comfort, and rested her head against the bark.

Lucas's anxiety touched her senses moments before his hand landed on her shoulder. He turned her to face him, and she averted her eyes. Dandelions poked their yellow heads between long blades of grass, and she studied them closely to avoid his heavy stare.

Why was she angry with him? There wasn't much he could have done to warn her, but he hadn't even looked at her. Something in that moment—when he had looked away—said so much about how alone she was in this whole situation.

"Hey." He pulled her chin up, and their eyes finally met. "We'll figure this out. I'll challenge Marcus—"

Fear made her stomach cramp, and she flinched. "No, you won't!"

His eyes widened. "What?"

"Don't do that, Lucas." Rosie grabbed his arms, clawing at his skin. "Please, promise me."

"Rosie, it's the only way—"

"No." Rosie shook her head. "I remember Dad telling me about him. He's huge. A beast. And he's mean. He said he was surprised Roger lived through it when he challenged him. Lucas, he'll kill you."

Lucas flinched, and anger flashed in his eyes. "Thanks for the vote of confidence."

"You know what I mean, Lucas." Rosie pressed on, undeterred by his deflection. "You're sixteen."

Lucas brushed Rosie's hands off his arms and moved away, running a hand through his hair. When he turned back, determination burned in his eyes. "It's the only thing I can do, Rosie."

"Someday, maybe." Rosie stepped forward and touched his arm again. "But not now. Defeating Marcus in a fight is just the beginning. What if you did defeat him? What are you going to do? Become alpha at sixteen? You're still in high school."

"But—"

"Please, Lucas, can we not talk about this anymore?" Rosie hugged herself. "I just don't want to think about any of it anymore. Not right now."

If the Council ordered her to be with Calvin, she would be taken away from everything she knew and loved. If she thought about it too much, it would eat her alive.

Lucas studied her then stepped forward, pulling her in for a hug. It was the comfort she needed and craved, and the flames settled back to their usual pleasant warmth. She rested her head against his chest and squeezed her eyes shut as she listened to his frantic heartbeat.

FIVE

ROSIE

SATURDAY MORNING, ROSIE WOKE EARLY. SHE
pulled her blankets up to her chin as she cast her gaze
out the window. Under a clear blue sky, light from the
rising sun filtered through the trees and promised a
beautiful day. Tempting as it was to stay under her
soft nest of blankets, she pushed them back and slid
out of bed.

She padded across the floor to the small balcony
and pushed the French doors open. Cool air brushed
over her, washing away the sleepy haze that still clung
to her eyelids. Sun touched the crisp spikes of ever-
green poking through the top of the forest, and she
breathed in the fresh pine scent. Dewdrops on the
lawn sparkled. In the far corner of the yard, the
garden called to her. The patch of color stood out
among all the green of the pristinely manicured
hedges. A white picket fence encircled the space, and
a trellis laced with climbing honeysuckle marked the
inviting entrance. It had been ages since she'd given
the flowers some attention. Time in the garden would
be the perfect way to start her day.

Determined not to let the events of yesterday and

the uncertainty of her fate ruin her day, she closed her eyes and took a deep, calming breath.

She stepped back into her room, shuffled across the floor, and grabbed her watering can. She made her way around the room quickly, watering her plants and watching them perk with the energy from her touch. It would be a warm day, so when she stepped into her closet, she chose a pair of shorts and a tee, but she also grabbed a hoodie to ward off the cold morning air. She could ditch it later.

She stepped softly down the stairs. The house was quiet—a change from the normal chaos of living with a handful of energetic boys. Later in the day, there would be the usual shouted insults and stomping up and down the stairs and loud televisions and hoots and hollers. Now, as everyone slept, the house seemed to sigh in a moment of quiet relief, like a mother sipping coffee before her little hellions woke up.

After moving through the hallway and past the dining room, Rosie made her way outside and across the stone patio. She shivered as her bare feet met the cool, dewy grass, and she stepped quickly across the yard, beyond the labyrinth of hedges, to the large, gated garden.

A kaleidoscope of color met her as she stepped through the maze of flowering bushes. Pink, yellow, and blue blossoms popped open as her energy wafted over the perennials. When she approached the rose bushes, something seemed off with their energy, and she furrowed her brow. The wilted edges of decaying blooms emanated a gloomy vibe. She methodically plucked the dead flowers, and new ones magically re-placed them in seconds. Soon, the garden was thriving with fresh energy, and she smiled with satisfaction.

"I've been meaning to prune those roses. You beat me to it."

Rosie startled at the sound of Daniel's voice. With her hand over her heart, she exhaled, then she turned and gave her cousin a warm smile. Hedge clippers in one hand and gardening gloves in the other, he looked ready to tackle the bushes. His tousled dark hair, tanned skin, and tall, lean frame made him look like a movie star. Sometimes Rosie was sure she was the only one in her family not blessed with godlike beauty. Even her father's creepy cousin Amos would be devastatingly handsome if he didn't comb his hair to the side and dress like a nerd.

Daniel studied his hands. "Look, about yesterday. Rosie, we shouldn't have held a meeting without you. That wasn't right. I'm sorry."

"Thank you, Danny. That means a lot."

"And as far as the Cramers—"

"I really don't want to talk about it." Tears stung Rosie's eyes. Damn. So much for not letting it ruin her day. "The more we talk about it, the worse it will make me feel."

Daniel bobbed his head, his face the picture of unease.

"I didn't think you usually worked on Saturdays," Rosie said as he pulled on his gloves and got to work searching the rose bushes for anything Rosie had missed.

"I didn't get much done around here this week." He found a dead bud and trimmed it. "It rained the first half of the week, so we were already behind, then a couple of the guys got the flu. I've been mowing for two days."

Daniel and Michael worked together to manage the landscaping and maintenance of all the properties owned by the Hart family. Equipment was stored in a warehouse on a piece of Hart land outside town, and the two of them had offices there, where they managed the locals they hired to help with cleaning, general maintenance, mowing, weeding, planting, and mulching on the properties. The employees worked everywhere except Hart House. No one was allowed at Hart House unless invited.

"You should have asked us to help." Rosie ran her fingers over a rose bud and watched it open. "You know Sam, Lucas, and I would have pitched in."

Daniel shrugged. "I had it under control. It's your last week of summer vacation. You shouldn't spend it working in the—" Daniel whipped his head toward the forest. His nostrils flared as he tipped his nose up slightly.

"What is it?" Rosie looked out toward the trees. Unlike the other werewolves, Rosie's senses weren't heightened while in human form. All she could smell were flowers and pine.

"I thought I smelled one of the pack, but it was different. Is someone out for a run this morning?"

"I don't think so. It was really quiet when I left the house."

"Yeah." Daniel furrowed his brow before he turned back to Rosie. A smile replaced the pensive expression on his face. "Someone probably left their scent behind close to the house. I thought I heard a growl, though." He shook his head.

An uneasy feeling crept up Rosie's skin, making the hair on the back of her neck rise. She looked out to the trees again and contemplated shifting, just so she could use her wolf senses. Her stomach churning with tension, she shivered and ran her hands over her arms. They were being watched. She was sure of it. A malicious, angry energy lingered in the air around the trees.

The snap of a twig behind her caused her heart to shoot up to her throat, and she gasped as she spun toward the sound.

"Amos. You're up early." Daniel's cool voice drifted in the breeze, but Rosie's attention was on Amos. His red-brown eyes matched those of every other Hart family member, but they carried a malice that was only him. It emanated from him. His energy was always angry. His hatred for Rosie soured the air and made him unbearable to be around.

Rosie's breath caught in her throat as Amos held her gaze before shifting it toward the woods. His eyes glowed yellow—just for a moment—before they returned to their normal red-brown. Rosie almost missed the brief shift as his focus slid back to her.

"Seems I'm not the only one." Amos's voice was low and gravelly. His lip curled as he looked Rosie over. He didn't spare a glance in Daniel's direction as he responded to him. "Breakfast will be ready soon."

He turned and headed toward the house, his posture stiff.

"He's so creepy." Daniel's statement was punctuated by a humorless laugh.

"Yeah." Rosie could barely make her voice work as she watched Amos slowly move across the lawn. "What do you think he was doing out here?"

"Who knows. Probably out for a morning run. I'm guessing he's the one I heard out in the woods. It would make sense. Leave it to Amos to growl like a creepy stalker."

Rosie nodded with a wan smile, but it didn't make

sense. She felt the same chilly energy from Amos that she'd felt from the woods only a few moments ago, but how could he have gotten from the woods to the yard so quickly?

~

FLAMES BOUNCED from the crackling fire with a pop. Embers landed on the stone floor of the patio, where they flickered briefly before they cooled to black, charred pieces of ash. Beside Rosie, Michael laughed at something Sam had said, and his beer breath mingled with the campfire smell from the firepit.

As she pulled her blanket around her shoulders, she breathed in deeply and fought the urge to cough at the smoke that burned her throat. Her hands were toasty from holding them out to the fire, but she couldn't say the same for her legs. She lifted her feet from the ground and wrapped her hands around them.

"So, I ran into Hansen at Miller's last night." Michael took another sip of his beer. "Him and Gloria are having problems. He was bawling about it for about an hour. Wouldn't shut up about how much he missed her. He's staying with a friend."

"Yeah, Gloria stopped into the office to pick up her paycheck." Daniel's eyes widened as he spoke. "She said she kicked him out because he came home drunk again. She's worried about the kids."

Rosie had met Gloria once or twice. She worked for the family, cleaning cabins. One of her sons was in her class.

"I think their drunk dad is the last thing on the kids' minds." Sam laughed. "They're both out behind the bleachers, getting baked a couple times a week at least." He mimed sucking on a joint and laughed again.

And they said *women* gossiped. A group of teenage girls had nothing on her boys.

"Hey, did you guys see the tree that went down over the lower bank by the ravine last week?" Michael's face lit up. "It's propped on a rock and teeters a little bit. Makes a perfect springboard to jump the narrow strip of the river. I cleared the water all the way over to the other bank. All four paws hit dirt."

"Nice!" Sam's face glowed from the fire's heat. "I have to check that out. I slip on those damned rocks every time and end up taking a bath in the river."

"Water in the ravine is friggin' freezing." Daniel frowned. "I got chased in by a bobcat last week. The thing was fast. Couldn't shake him till I jumped in the water." When the boys all laughed, Daniel scowled. "Yeah, yeah. Funny."

"Damn." Michael wiped at a fake tear. "Wish I could have seen that."

Rosie was curled up in the patio chair with the thick blanket Lucas had brought out for her, and her core warmed from the relaxed, content energy of her favorite people.

Her eyes darted across the fire to Lucas. He stared at her with a funny smile.

"Warming up yet?" He spoke to her telepathically, something other werewolves could only do in wolf form. Since discovering their mate bond, they'd found they were also able to communicate that way in human form.

"Getting there," Rosie projected to him. The words sounded the same in their heads as they would if they'd been spoken aloud.

Flames danced in the firepit and cast a yellow glow over Lucas's face as he watched her. His gaze bored into her, stoking the fire deep inside her that she tried her hardest to keep contained. Since their fight yesterday, he'd been at her side almost constantly, and she was glad. She craved his presence, almost like her mate bond had intensified. Become stronger. Suddenly, the desire to touch him—to feel him—was overwhelming.

He rolled his lips inward and straightened in his chair. "*Meet me at your tree.*"

Could he read her thoughts now too?

"Well, boys," Lucas said, and all eyes turned from the fire to him. "It's time for me to go to bed."

Making a show of stretching her arms above her head and yawning, Rosie stood from her chair. "I need to go to bed too. You guys wore me out."

Skepticism. That would be the best way to describe the energy she felt. They knew something was up. Whether it was just Sam—he was looking at her with a crooked grin—or Daniel and Michael suspected as well, she didn't know. They wouldn't say anything if they knew something was going on anyway.

Right?

Rosie took one last look at Lucas before she turned and headed into the house, pretending to make her way to bed. Instead, she shifted course and moved through the kitchen and down the small hallway that led to the cook's kitchen. In the small area where Martha spent much of her time, a doorway to the right led to the basement. To the left was an exit to the side of the house.

She tiptoed to the door and opened it. She would need to be quiet. Hopefully, the boys wouldn't distinguish her steps from the sounds of the hundreds of other creatures that roamed at night. Their loud voices and boisterous laughs drowned out most of the sounds of the forest.

A pitch-black expanse lay before her, but she didn't hesitate as she leaped forward at a full run. The yard and miles of forest beyond were more familiar to her than the back of her hand. She sprinted across the cool grass until she reached the trees. Pausing by her oak, she touched the bark and felt its answering vibration before she knelt on the ground and waited.

Every cell in her body screamed in anticipation. In the beginning, just being near Lucas had been enough. As time passed, her innocent crush grew to primal desire. How long could she fight the needs of the wolf inside her?

Minutes later, the sound of feet shuffling through the grass made her heart race, and she held her breath. Lucas dropped to his knees in front of her and took her face into his hands as he pressed his lips firmly to hers. Anticipation turned to immediate gratification. Like an itch being scratched, his touch elicited a wash of pleasure through her body.

The beginning was rough as they each clawed their way to each other, trying to get closer, needing to satisfy the desire embedded deep inside. As they sank to the earth, their kisses softened. Tender. A breathy sigh escaped Rosie's lips.

After several minutes, Rosie leaned back and huffed out a contented breath. She could barely make out his outline in the dark, but she could feel his presence and clung to it like a child to a security blanket.

His fingers traced over her cheek, and she closed her eyes. Having his skin against hers brought so much more pleasure than she'd ever thought she could experience. He traced a finger down the bridge of her nose, to her mouth. He paused there before moving down her chin, past her neck, to her chest. He put his hand over her heart then pulled her to him, hugging her close.

They stayed like that, lying still in the dark, until she fell asleep.

SIX

ROSIE

After Michael detailed, washed, and tuned up the Jeep Wrangler, it looked better than if it had been driven right off the car sales lot. A pine-tree-shaped air freshener dangled from the rearview mirror, giving the interior that new-car scent.

Rosie sensed sadness from Michael as he stood next to her in the garage. A white muscle shirt showed off his bulging biceps and broad chest. His brow knit, and he bit his lip as he eyed the Jeep before slowly handing the keys over. "Take good care of her, Rosie. She's a spitfire."

"Are you sure you're okay with this, Michael?" Rosie took the keys from her cousin then tossed her backpack onto the back seat.

Michael took a deep breath and eyed the vehicle again. He placed his hands on his hips and nodded. "Yeah. Betty will take good care of you."

"Betty?"

"Yes. Her name is Betty. Be nice to her, and she'll be nice to you." Michael sniffed. "I had a talk with her, and she promises to keep you safe."

When Rosie stifled a laugh, Michael's eyes widened in mock horror.

"Don't you dare laugh. Have I ever laughed at you when you talk to your plants?"

Her jaw dropped. "How do you know about that?"

"Everyone knows you talk to flowers and trees and animals. You're weird. We roll with it." He gently punched her arm but then flashed a smile and pulled her into a one-armed hug. "And it's why we love you so much."

Lucas strolled into the garage with Sam trailing along behind him. He looked at the Jeep and raised an eyebrow. "So, who am I riding with?"

"Uh-uh." Sam shook his head of blond curls. "Not me. It's my senior year. *My* SUV is now being used to pick up chicks. I can't do that with you riding shotgun."

"Sam, you're such a pig." Rosie laughed. "Come on, Lucas. I need you to help me figure out what all the buttons do."

Lucas climbed into the passenger seat, and Rosie slid in behind the wheel. The engine started up with a low roar, and she gave Michael one last wave as she hit the gas. The Jeep lurched forward, the large tires screeching against the concrete floor. Sam's cackle echoed off the walls of the garage. Wincing, Rosie glanced at Michael and frowned as he covered his face with his hands and turned toward the house. Beside her, Lucas laughed, and she shot him a dirty look.

Hitting the gas a little more gently this time, she pulled out of the garage, down the driveway, and onto the road. The big Jeep jostled with each bump—a startling difference from the smooth ride of the Explorer.

"How are you doing? For real?" Lucas ran a hand down her arm.

Rosie sighed. "I'm still not going to talk about the Cramers. And I'm not looking forward to today." The first day of school always sucked. The air was thick with first-day jitters, and everyone's nerves weighed heavily on her. She typically spent the day hiding behind her headphones.

He squeezed her arm, and a familiar tingle ran through her. It had become like a drug. She couldn't get enough of it.

"We have our first two periods together," he said soothingly. "I'll be right beside you."

She met his gaze, and her breath caught at the warmth and determination in his eyes. Lucas was the one person in the world whose emotions she couldn't read, but she was learning she didn't *need* to read them. She could feel his love with every look, every touch. It filled her with something she'd never known she was missing. She reached for his hand, and he grasped hers, squeezing tightly.

They rolled into Hanks Hollow, and Rosie marveled at the beauty of their little town as the rising sun cast a glow over the buildings settled between the tree-covered bluffs and the glittering lake. She steered the Jeep into the high school parking lot and found a spot toward the back.

Rosie turned the Jeep off, and Lucas gave a visual sweep of the area before he leaned forward and brushed a soft kiss over her lips. Holding her breath in anticipation, she kissed him back, running a hand gently over his cheek.

He frowned after he pulled away. "*I hate having to keep this a secret.*"

"*Me too.*" Rosie projected. "*It's going to be so hard not to reach for your hand. I hate not being able to touch you.*"

He ran a finger gently down the bridge of her nose. *"After school. We'll go out for a hike."*

Rosie nodded then turned her stare to the school building. A knot formed in her stomach. "It's going to be a long day."

Lucas nudged her shoulder. "Come on."

They made their way across the lot toward the little redbrick building. Rosie focused on the trees that towered in the distance and silently wished she could escape to the forest.

After they pushed their way through the glass doors, Rosie hesitantly pried herself away from Lucas's side to go find her locker. She winced at the clamor of students in the hall as she searched for locker number sixty-two. After she found it, she read the combination on her registration form and concentrated on the task of manipulating the little lock. It opened with a jerk, and she deposited some of her school supplies inside.

She searched her schedule for the room number for her sociology class and dodged her way through throngs of kids. After finding it, she beelined to the back of the room and slid into an empty desk. The anxiety in the air prickled her skin like cactus needles, and she reached for her headphones.

As her fingers closed around them, she heard Lucas's soft voice in her head.

"Hey, beautiful."

Their eyes met as he slid into the seat across from her. The needle-sharp emotions in the room fell away.

"Did you see Cassie Barnes? She's wearing enough makeup to cover all the contestants in a beauty pageant."

Stifling a giggle, she turned to the seat in front of Lucas, where Cassie was playing with her long dark hair. Sure enough, her face was caked with a thick layer of foundation that was a couple of shades darker than her complexion. It looked like she'd smeared peanut butter over her cheeks. Yikes.

A tinge of guilt hit Rosie, but she pushed it away. Cassie had teased her relentlessly since the second grade.

Cassie pinned Rosie with a cold stare. "What are you looking at, Freak Show?" Her gaze trailed over to Lucas, and she gave a coy smile. "Hi, Lucas."

Nope. Not feeling guilty. Rosie averted her eyes and hid a small smile as Lucas muffled a laugh. And just like that, her anxiety melted away.

Second period was just as easy. Rosie found she didn't need to use her headphones once. She drew strength from Lucas, relaxing with the soothing sounds of his voice when he spoke to her telepathically.

During third period, her free period, she sat outside on the terrace and was pleasantly surprised when she heard his voice in her head. He was all the way on the other side of the school. How far could their projections reach? It was something they would need to experiment with.

It was fourth period when things took a serious nosedive.

After a quick stop at her locker to grab a book, Rosie made her way to Mr. McCall's classroom. She stepped inside and took inventory of the students who had already arrived. Two-person tables were neatly arranged into two rows. Dread swept over her. She loathed lab classes. Aside from science not being her thing, she hated being assigned a partner. She almost never ended up with someone she knew.

Slowly moving toward the back of the room, Rosie

picked up on snippets of conversations about summer vacation and first-day classes. She found an empty table and sat, heaving her backpack up and setting it in front of her. As she absently ran a finger over the stitching on the side of the bag, she opened herself to the energy in the room. A mix of emotions smacked into her. Nervousness. Excitement.

A shadow moved over her desk, carrying a bitter energy that left a bad taste in her mouth. Arrogance. Anger. When she jerked her head up, her eyes locked onto Mason Lewis. His large frame towered over her, and he stared at her with cold blue eyes. Dread settled in her stomach, and she swallowed thickly.

"How's it going, Hart?" A smug grin tugged at his lips.

Instead of answering, she tore her backpack open and reached inside for her headphones. With shaky fingers, she fastened them over her ears. Even with them on, she heard his malicious chuckle. It tore at something inside her. Deep breaths, in through her nose and out through her mouth, did little to settle the painful burn of anxiety in her stomach. He smirked and turned to take a seat at one of the other tables.

"*Rosie?*" She almost didn't hear the sweet voice over the hammering of her heart.

"*Lucas!*" The desperation in her tone made her cringe. Way to be strong.

"*What is it? What's wrong?*"

"*It's Mason. He's in my biology class.*"

After a beat of silence, his voice returned, soothing and soft. "*Just focus on me, Rosie. Ignore him. He's nothing. Listen to my voice.*"

Rosie closed her eyes.

"*I'm in trig. First day, and I'm willing to bet we'll get a pile of homework. Mr. Adams is such a dick.*"

The acidic bubbles of anxiety in her stomach started to dissolve, and Rosie took a deep breath. Even in her head, the sound of her voice was shaky. *"I don't think trigonometry will be included in my high school career. I barely passed algebra last year."*

"Meh. Who needs math? It's overrated."

Rosie opened her eyes as Mr. McCall strolled into the classroom and started writing on the board. She took her headphones off and slipped them back into her backpack.

"Okay, everyone. I hope you all had a good summer. Don't get too comfortable. I'm going to be moving you as I do roll call." The teacher spoke as he moved to his iPad and picked it up off his desk. "When I call your name, take a seat at the table number I assign to you."

"Doing okay, Rosie?" Lucas's soft voice filled her head again.

"Yeah." Rosie took another deep breath as she glanced at Mason out of the corner of her eye. He was sitting with his back to her, and she fought the urge to throw something at him. *"I'm good."*

"I'm right here when you need me."

Mr. McCall started calling out names and table numbers. Her attention went back to the stitching on her bag until she heard her name.

"Rose Hart. Ah! Any relation to Sam Hart?"

Rosie was used to this. Sammy was popular with both the students and the teachers. Everyone loved her brother. The disappointment that came when others realized she was nothing like him irritated her. She nodded slowly to his question and waited patiently for him to assign her to her seat.

"Let's hope you're a little less of a clown than Sam." Mr. McCall sounded annoyed, and Rosie smiled as she imagined her brother's disrupting antics. A low hum of laughter went through the classroom. Her classmates knew her as the quiet freak, a far cry from the class clown. "Okay, Rose. You're at table ten."

The chair screeched as she stood, and she slowly picked up her backpack and made her way to table ten. It wasn't at the back of the classroom, but at least it was close to the window. As she sat down, her gaze drifted to the tree line that bordered the football field. In her mind, she let herself wander through the rows of birch and pine, listening to the wind blow through the leaves. Distantly, she could hear Mr. McCall continuing to assign seats, and nerves danced in her stomach. The table-ten assignment would seal her fate for the remainder of the term. Instead of trying to stay invisible until the bell rang, she would be forced to interact each day with her lab partner. She prayed it was someone she was at least somewhat familiar with. She knew a few of Becca's closest friends and talked to them from time to time. Some of them were in the classroom, so hopefully, one of them...

"Table ten."

Surprise fluttered in her heart. Whose name had Mr. McCall just called out? As she turned her head, her breath caught in her throat, and she watched in horror as Mason Lewis stood from his chair and made his way toward her.

SEVEN

ROSIE

"*What?*" Becca's eyes rounded, her blue irises trained on Rosie with horror. "Maybe you can ask Mr. McCall if you can switch partners."

"I already tried that." Rosie poked at her chicken nuggets. Hunger made her stomach ache. Or maybe it was nerves. Either way, she wasn't sure she could keep any food down. Not now. "Mr. McCall asked if there was a problem with Mason. If he had done something to make me uncomfortable. I froze. What was I supposed to say? I wasn't going to tell him the truth. He said if I couldn't give him a valid reason, he wouldn't move me."

"Oh, that really sucks." It was stating the obvious, but the defeat in Becca's voice captured the moment perfectly. "You know, if it makes you feel better, half the school doesn't believe anything he says. They know he's a lying snake."

"That's nice to hear, Becca. Thanks."

Rosie didn't bother telling her it really didn't help her at all. She couldn't care less what half the school thought. It didn't make sitting next to him any easier. What were the odds of being assigned as his lab partner *again*? She'd gotten to know him last year when they were lab partners in their sopho-more science class. He'd been charming and sweet, winning her over when he told her he loved the same wildlife websites and blogs she enjoyed reading.

"What's with the sour faces?" Sam plopped down in the seat across from Rosie and reached for one of her chicken nuggets.

Rosie slapped his hand away.

"Ouch! Rude!"

"Hi, Sam." Becca straightened in her seat and brushed a hand through her hair.

Rosie had to fight an eye roll at the adoration and lust that poured from her friend. Becca's crush on Sam was obvious to everyone in the world except Sam.

"Rosie's having a bad day. Mason Lewis got as-signed as her partner in biology."

"What?" Sam's hand froze over the chicken nugget on Rosie's plate. "Where is he? I'll kick his ass right now."

"No, you won't." Rosie furrowed her brow. "I don't want a repeat of what happened last time. No more police stations and black eyes. Besides, he hasn't technically done anything." She sighed at the raised eyebrow and incredulous stare from her brother. "Nothing new, anyway. I can handle this myself."

Sam opened his mouth, ready to object, but Rosie grabbed his hand, sending a calming vibe through her fingers. He stopped, the creases on his forehead evap-orating as the tension left his face.

"I need to handle this myself, Sam. Please let me. Stay away from him."

"*Does that go for me too?*" Lucas appeared behind Sam, projecting his voice into Rosie's head. "*Because*

I've been fantasizing about running his head into a concrete wall for the past hour."

"That goes for you too. Please, Lucas. Leave it alone."

Lucas nodded as he set his tray beside Sam and took a seat. He swatted the back of Sam's head when he tried to swipe a chicken nugget off his plate. "Seriously, dude. Get your own."

"Did you see the line? No way I'm waiting ten minutes for some cold chicken nuggets."

"Here." Rosie slid her tray to Sam. "I don't think I can eat right now."

~

AFTER SCHOOL, once Rosie was home, she beelined to her oak tree in the backyard. Its energy enveloped her like strong arms as she leaned against it, running her hand down the rough bark. Leaf-covered branches brushed against her cheek, wiping away tears she hadn't realized were there.

After sliding to the ground, she rested against the solid trunk and closed her eyes. It didn't take long until she felt the tickle of tiny feet running up her leg. She opened her eyes and greeted her squirrel friends. They'd grown over the summer. No longer the babies she remembered from the springtime. Still, they seemed to be drawn to the area, making their home in her oak and never straying far. Every time she visited her spot, her friends were nearby.

One crawled into her lap and circled three times before curling up, a comforting weight against her thigh. Chirps pierced the air above her as the other three squirrels chased one another up and down the trunk. Chunks of bark flew away from their lightning-fast feet and into Rosie's hair.

Moments later, approaching footsteps crunched over twigs and leaves. The squirrels scattered just as Rosie heard her favorite voice come from behind.

"I thought I'd find you out here." Lucas smiled down at her as he approached. "You disappeared so fast after we got home that I was afraid maybe I'd done something wrong."

"I just needed to be alone for a few minutes." As much as she loved Lucas, Rosie also craved solitude from time to time, even if it made the mate bond uncomfortable. "I haven't forgotten our date."

She patted her oak goodbye then took Lucas's hand. They stepped farther into the forest, under the cover of trees. After walking a few yards, Lucas spun her around and caught her in his arms, leaning down to brush his lips over hers. She melted into his embrace.

The taste of his lips, rich but with a hint of mint, was welcome and familiar. He always smelled clean. Like soap and shampoo and fresh deodorant, but underneath all that was a scent that was just him. Just Lucas. She drew a deep breath in through her nose, taking him in.

Every time sweet contentment overtook her, the dark clouds of William Cramer's threat rolled in, ruining everything. She'd managed to convince everyone to stop talking about it, but she couldn't force her brain to stop thinking about it. No matter how hard she tried.

"Are you okay?" Lucas's eyes searched hers, and she couldn't lie.

"I'm trying to be."

"We can—"

Her finger went to his mouth. "If it happens. *If.* I don't want my last moments with you to be spent talking about it. I want them to be happy. Besides, the Council made it sound like they wanted this to be in a few years. Not like... now. Hopefully they'll tell William to back off."

A frown creased Lucas's features before he forced a smile and nodded. "You're probably right."

Rosie pulled him down for a long kiss then broke away. "Of course I'm right."

They spent the next hour lying in the grass, talking and kissing.

But the fleeting moments weren't nearly enough. Lucas took out his phone and gave a defeated sigh. "It's time for dinner."

Pack dinners were at the same time every night, and attendance was required. Rosie pouted as they rose from the ground and headed toward the house.

The rest of the pack was already seated around the table when they entered the dining room.

"There you kids are," Martha called as she carried a bowl of pasta from the kitchen and set it on the large oak dining table. "I thought I was going to have to come out to find you."

Heat rose to Rosie's cheeks, and she spoke softly. "We wanted to get our hike in for the day. No more morning walks. We'll have to do it after school now."

A small smile quirked Sam's lips as he eyed Rosie. He met her eyes and touched the side of his head, picking at his hair. She took the hint and quickly touched her curls, finding a few leaves, which she plucked out and tossed to the floor. Her cheeks heated even more as she glanced around the room. Thank God, no one else seemed to notice.

"I'm glad you've found a hobby outside of books

and electronics, Lucas," Roger said gruffly as he spooned some mashed potatoes onto his plate and winked. "Rosie is a good influence on you."

"Maybe I should join you guys on one of your hikes," Daniel said casually as he stabbed at a piece of broccoli on his plate. "It sounds like fun."

Exchanging glances with Lucas, Rosie flashed a smile. "Of course. Just let us know when you'd like to come along."

"Come on, Daniel." Sam scoffed. "You spend all day outside, getting exercise. You're not going to abandon our Mario Kart time to go on a nature walk, are you? I've already lost Lucas to the great outdoors. Don't tell me I'm going to lose you now too."

Daniel jumped in his chair, and his eyes rounded before he pinned Sam with a confused glare, mouthing, "Ow," and rubbing his leg.

Rosie's eyes darted to her father, sure he'd picked up on the obvious kick Sam had given Daniel, but Simon was busy cutting up the meat on his plate.

He set his fork down and took a breath before glancing at Michael. His brow furrowed. "I heard from the Legacy Agency today."

Silence filled the room. The Legacy Agency, run by a group of werewolves in Canada, specialized in providing egg donation and surrogate services for werewolves. Since werewolves had historically only been men, finding women to mother new generations —while keeping the existence of werewolves a secret —was challenging.

"You can relax, Michael," Simon continued. "You're not a father yet. The insemination didn't take. They'll try again next month."

Michael's shoulders drooped. Whether it was in relief or disappointment, Rosie wasn't sure. He was hard to read sometimes. He didn't like to take any-thing seriously. His muscular build looked intimidat-ing, but he was a teddy bear—unless provoked. Then he turned into a temperamental, foot-stomping, tantrum-throwing toddler.

Although Michael would be the child's biological father, the pack would raise it together. Just as had been done with the other children, Martha would provide the nurturing parts while the pack taught it the ways of the werewolves.

The Legacy Agency was fairly new. Until a few generations ago, it had been common for werewolves to find an outcast, hunt her down, impregnate her, then lock her up while she carried the baby. After the woman gave birth, the pack *ate* her. Hart House still had prison cells in the basement. Rosie shivered as she recalled what she'd recently learned. Her gaze went to her great-uncle Stuart. He glanced at her but averted his eyes quickly. She swallowed her tears as she felt his sadness and guilt.

It was Amos who told her. Stuart just confirmed it as truth. After Rosie's grandmother gave birth to her father, Stuart joined in as they feasted on her body. She still couldn't look at the quiet, kind, gentle man in the same way. Memories of the years she'd spent in his lap, listening to his stories, were tainted by the image of him killing a human. Her *grandmother*.

In recent years, many werewolves had adopted the practice of using surrogates, but a number of werewolves still balked at the idea. Her father's cousin Amos was one of those who thought the idea of a surrogate was absurd. Rosie could feel his fury from across the table. Sitting ramrod straight in his chair, he ran a hand over his neatly combed hair. His clothes were pristine, his manners impeccable, his attitude hostile. He was determined to hold to the traditional way of doing things, no matter how barbaric it was. And he hated Rosie. He'd once called her an abomination. That word, that *label*, hung over her head like a dark cloud.

The Cramers were famous for the way they held so strongly to the barbaric past of werewolves. They refused to use the surrogate agency, and they went through dozens of women for help around their house. Since humans were forbidden to exist outside a pack house with knowledge of the werewolf world, Rosie could only guess what they did to the poor women when they were through with them.

Her stomach tightened when she thought about the possibility that she could be forced to stay with them. Her gaze trailed over to Lucas. He picked at his food, looking deep in thought. As though feeling her eyes on him, he looked up. As if a switch had flipped, she felt safe. The thought of leaving him brought a throbbing pain in her heart.

EIGHT

ROSIE

One of Rosie's favorite songs blasted through the Jeep's speakers during the drive to school the next morning, but she couldn't focus on the tune. No matter how hard she tried not to think about the Cramers, her thoughts stayed on them.

She glanced at her lap, where Lucas held her hand. He squeezed his fingers tightly around hers, and she squeezed back.

"You okay?" Lucas used his other hand to turn the radio down.

"I am right now. But in general, not so much. I just wish..."

"I know." Lucas squeezed her hand again. "Me too."

When they got to school, Rosie set a slow pace through the parking lot. Even with Lucas's long strides, he stayed with her. After they pushed through the front doors, they parted ways to go to their lockers.

They met again in sociology class minutes later, sliding into seats at the back of the classroom. As the teacher droned on about Pavlov's dogs, Rosie found it hard to concentrate. With her future on the line, school felt trivial. When Cassie flashed a smile at

Lucas for the fifth or sixth time, Rosie had to fight the urge to pummel her. Territorial anger festered deep inside. She dug her nails into her hands as she gritted her teeth.

Rosie had managed to push anxiety over fourth period to the back of her mind until she neared the door to the biology classroom. Her heart hammered as she stepped inside and found Mason already seated at their table. He'd chosen the aisle seat. While she was happy to have the window seat, that meant she had to slide past him to get there.

As she neared the table, he scooted his chair back, giving her a narrow area to fit through. He smirked at her when she shimmied behind him. She was almost through when he turned and put his hand on the back of his chair, raising his fingers so they brushed against her breasts.

The room closed in on her, and her breath caught in her throat. Something snapped, and months of pent-up aggression poured from her as she slapped him as hard as she could. The shock on his face caused a euphoric tingle of satisfaction in her skin, and the words were out of her mouth before she could stop them. "Keep your filthy hands off me, pervert!"

His eyes rounded, and he leaned back. Silence filled the room for a fraction of a second before laughter erupted. His cheeks reddened, and he threw his hands up in surrender.

Thankfully, the teacher hadn't yet arrived, or Rosie was sure she would be spending the rest of her days in detention.

"You got it, freak." His words were dismissive as he turned his back to her, but she felt his humiliation.

Something shifted, and her shoulders felt lighter. A weight he'd placed there months ago had lightened.

It was still there—it would always be there—but a tiny ray of hope made her breathe a little easier. For the first time in forever, she felt a small sense of control.

~

"It was so great!" Squeezing the steering wheel tightly, Rosie bounced up and down in the driver's seat. "Lucas, I wish you could have seen his face. Mason didn't say a word to me the rest of class. He didn't look at me once. No more of those stupid asshole smiles. *Smack!*" Rosie mimed a slapping motion.

Lucas laughed and placed a kiss on her cheek. "I wish I could have seen it."

The gate to Hart House came into view, and Rosie pressed the automatic gate opener. The large iron gate opened slowly, and she steered the Jeep up the long, tree-lined driveway. As they reached the top, where the concrete path circled around to the front of the house, Rosie spotted an unfamiliar SUV parked in front of the sidewalk that led to the front door.

"Who's that?" Lucas pointed at the SUV.

Rosie shrugged. "I don't know."

After parking in the garage, Rosie grabbed her backpack and swung it over her shoulder as she climbed out of the Jeep. She joined Lucas outside the garage, and they made their way up the stone stairs to the veranda.

Lucas tensed when Rosie's hand went for the front door, and he placed a hand over hers. She started to ask what was wrong, but the tilt of his head answered her. His sensitive wolf hearing had picked up something she couldn't hear.

"*What is it?*" she asked.

The worry in Lucas's blue eyes was hard to miss. *"It's the Council."*

A sinking feeling settled in Rosie's stomach, and she took a step back, ready to make a break for it.

"Too late," Lucas projected. *"They know you're here. They're waiting for you. Your father—"*

Rosie's father opened the front door. "Rosie. We've been waiting for you. Come inside."

NINE

LUCAS

Lucas hadn't been invited to this conversation, but he edged his way into the living room and sat on one of the armchairs by the window. Everyone's focus was on Rosie, so no one seemed to notice or care about him. He sat numbly, placing his backpack on the floor next to him.

She looked so small as Simon took her backpack from her and steered her to one of the two large leather couches that sat on either side of the immense fireplace. The three Council members were seated on one, their backs to Lucas, and Sam sat on the other, facing him. His eyes flitted to Lucas for a fraction of a second before they trained on Rosie.

Rosie's hands shook as she sat down between Sam and Simon. She tucked a chunk of her red curls behind her ear, and she bit her lip.

Something was squeezing his chest, restricting his ability to breathe properly. The urge to run to her was almost more than he could take.

"Rose." Jagger spoke first. The large, muscular man looked like he'd stepped off a Brawny paper towel commercial. He definitely had an Alaskan-wilderness look to him. Lucas could barely hear him over the pounding of his heart. "We're here to talk to you about William Cramer's recent request. Your father tells us he's shared with you that William wishes for you to court his son."

Rosie's porcelain skin paled to nearly translucent as she nodded slowly.

"I realize it sounds old-fashioned," Garrett cut in. His long, sandy hair and laid-back vibe spoke of his coastal roots. He represented the Pacific Northwest region, where packs were known to be a bit more progressive. "But it's not a horrible idea."

Lucas was going to be sick. He watched her close her eyes.

"*Lucas...*"

He couldn't breathe as her voice came into his head. "*I'm here, Rosie. I'm right here.*"

"*Take me out of here, Lucas. Please.*" When she opened her eyes again, a tear spilled down her cheek.

"Oh, please, girl," Roland growled. "Spare us the dramatics."

Lucas wanted to strangle the pompous old man. His wavy silver locks were combed neatly, and unlike the other two council members, he was pristine. A tailored suit. Pompous, just like William. A true Cramer.

"Rose," Jagger said again. "We're not forcing you to join his pack. Not yet. Right now, we just think it would be a good idea for you to get to know him. That's all. You'll stay with the Cramers on the weekends. During the week, you'll remain here with your pack."

Relief poured through Lucas, but tension lingered. Thank God, Rosie wouldn't have to join the Cramer pack. But she wasn't out of the woods.

"It's not a request," Roland cut in. He scowled at

the easy way Jagger talked to Rosie. "We conferred and made a decision. You will do as you're told. If you don't, you'll answer to us. You know we don't take prisoners or give second chances. Punishment for disobeying the Council is death."

"They know that, Roland." Garrett crossed his arms. "Everyone knows that. However, she's the only female werewolf we have. Werewolves all over the world are watching and waiting to see what happens. We can't just kill her." He furrowed his brow. "But trust me. If you know what's good for you, you'll do what you're told."

Simon placed a hand on Rosie's shoulder. "When?"

When Roland answered, the blood in Lucas's veins turned to ice. "The Cramers are expecting her there Saturday morning for her first weekend visit."

"Dad!" Lucas pounded impatiently on his father's bedroom door. The moment it opened, Lucas pushed past him, slamming the door shut behind him. "I'm ready. I'm ready to challenge Marcus. Let's go. Let's do this."

Roger's eyes widened. He held his hands up in a calming gesture. "Whoa, son. Slow down."

"They're doing it. They're forcing Rosie on Calvin Cramer. I need to be an alpha. They have to choose me."

It was risky having this conversation in the house. Any one of the Harts could overhear. He didn't care.

"Lucas, you're not ready."

"Bullshit! You said..." His voice wavered, and

Lucas cursed. "You and Shawn both said I was doing well. That I was going to be a good alpha."

"You will make a good alpha, Lucas." Roger pushed him onto his bed and sat down next to him. "When you're older. You're sixteen, kid. You're not ready."

"I have to be ready, Dad." All he could think about was Rosie's plea to get her out of this mess. He wanted to. He wanted to so badly it caused a burning pain in the pit of his stomach.

"I'm sorry, Lucas." Roger placed a hand on his shoulder.

His father was right. He was still in high school. He wasn't ready to be an alpha. Not yet. Frustration clawed at him, and he fought the urge to scream. He ran his hands through his hair and clasped his fingers together atop his head.

"I've seen the way that girl looks at you, Lucas." Roger smiled. "Being forced to get to know this Calvin kid isn't going to change how she feels about you."

"But they're vile people, Dad. The thought of her having to spend time with them alone, unprotected..."

"There's nothing you can do about that," Roger said sadly. "But you know her father will step in if things go south for her. If the Cramers are smart, they'll be on their best behavior. The Council is watching. Simon is watching."

Nodding, Lucas took a calming breath. Everything would be okay. He had to believe that. Rosie would be looking to him for comfort. For strength.

He would do whatever it took to make her feel safe.

TEN

ROSIE

Jars of oil lined Clara's kitchen table, and Rosie methodically did as her grandma instructed, stuffing dried lavender into them and screwing on the lids. Her Wednesday time with her grandma had moved to late afternoon, after school, but she was determined to keep up the visits every week.

"We'll let these soak for a few weeks, then we'll have some nice lavender-infused oil to bottle and sell," Grandma said, filling jars along with Rosie. She paused and took a deep breath. "Want to tell me what's on your mind?"

Yesterday's bombshell still had Rosie reeling. Her relief over not immediately being forced to join the Cramer pack was overshadowed by the dread of a fast-approaching Saturday. She'd wordlessly retreated to her bedroom after the Council left. Ignoring Martha's pleas to come to dinner, she'd stayed in her room all night, wallowing in self-pity. Shame heated her cheeks. That had been childish and no doubt caused her father more stress and worry.

This morning, Lucas had spoken to her as though nothing was wrong, and Sam made jokes about her visit to the house of Creepy McCreeperson. They made her promise not to become a pod person. They were trying to make her feel better, and she appreciated their efforts.

Whether or not to tell her grandma about her impending visits with the Cramers had been weighing heavily on Rosie's mind all afternoon. Clara would know she was holding something back if she chose to keep it from her, but listening to her drone on about the evils of the misogynistic werewolf world was the last thing she needed right now.

"Spill it, Rose."

Rosie's back straightened at her grandmother's tone. "The Council ordered me to start visiting the Cramers every weekend."

"The Cramers? You mean the other werewolf pack? The ones who visited last spring?" After Rosie nodded, Clara narrowed her eyes. "Why?"

Averting her gaze, Rosie focused on the task of dunking dried petals into the oil. She shrugged. "They want Calvin and I to, like...date. Or something."

"*What?*"

Rosie tore her gaze away from the lavender to stare at her grandma.

"Those pompous—"

"Grandma, please. I know how messed up it is. What can I do? I have to do what they tell me."

"What is your father doing about this?"

"What can he do?" Rosie shrugged again. "It's the Council, Grandma."

Clara stood and moved to the window. Posture rigid, she crossed her arms. "We'll leave."

"What?"

"We'll move away. Somewhere with no werewolves. Florida, maybe. When's the last time you saw a wolf on a beach?"

Rosie swallowed the lump in her throat. Her grandma wasn't one to run away from problems. Her words were unsettling. "Grandma, you know I can't do that."

Being the voice of reason wasn't something she was used to. Tears welled in her eyes, and she took a deep breath, willing them away.

Clara's shoulders sagged in defeat, but she didn't move from her spot at the window. She kept her gaze fixed outside. "I know. Running away isn't the answer. I'm sorry." After a short pause, she continued, her voice unsteady. "But don't let that boy touch you, Rosie. You stay strong. No matter how much they talk down to you, remember how powerful and wonderful you are."

"Okay, Grandma."

"Good." She sniffed.

Was her grandma crying?

"Now finish up those jars. I'm going to go meditate. Talk of your werewolf world always gives me a headache."

Clara's tension came in waves, and Rosie absorbed her emotion. Helplessness...fear. She thought about her grandma's words the last time they'd spoken. The reality slammed into her with a force that made her want to cry. For the first time ever, her grandma didn't know how to help her. Loneliness that felt so much like the loneliness she felt the day she'd walked in on the pack meeting came over her. She felt it every time she imagined leaving Lucas—living without the comfort of their mate bond. Everything she held dear was being ripped from her.

THE SUN still lit the sky when Rosie left her grandma's, so she decided to take a detour into town and visit Becca at Miller's. Her father gave her permission to miss supper Wednesday nights when she visited her grandmother, so she could grab something to eat there. Things were getting heavy, and she needed her friend's carefree energy to lighten her mood.

She steered the Jeep up Main Street to the top of the park, where it met Lake Street, which was lined with parking spots for the businesses along the lakefront. She parked in front of Miller's, but rather than going in through the Lake Street entrance of the restaurant, she walked through the alley that led to the boardwalk.

As she stepped onto the wood-planked walkway that ran along Mingan Lake, a cool breeze touched her face. It smelled of lake water and pine from the forests that lay beyond. Rosie closed her eyes, soaking it in.

She made her way to Miller's boardwalk entrance. The large picture window with Miller's Bar and Grill etched in gold lettering greeted her as she approached. She opened the door, and music and the low hum of laughter and talking filled the air.

As she stepped inside, her gaze roamed over the people enjoying dinner in the dining room. To the right, the bar stretched the length of the wall. Above the rows of liquor bottles, the immense picture window gave the patrons sitting on barstools a lovely view of the lake. Even on a Wednesday evening, Miller's drew a crowd.

"Rosie!"

She swiveled back toward the dining room. Becca skipped toward her, carrying a tray in one hand and a notepad in the other. Her blond hair was tied in a neat ponytail on top of her head, and a black apron was tied around the waistband of her jean shorts. Her T-shirt with Miller's Bar and Grill written on it looked a size too small, accentuating her full bosom. "Flaunt it if you got it," as Becca would say.

"Hi, Becca," Rosie said shyly.

Her friend threw her arms around her as though they hadn't seen each other in years—they'd been together in school only a few hours earlier. "Looks like you're still working. Sorry. I should have texted first. I just wanted to drop in and say hi."

"I just have a couple of tables left, then we can eat, if you haven't yet."

"Sounds good. I'm starving."

"Great! Plant your tooshie at the bar, and talk to my dad while I finish up."

Feeling her mood lighten exponentially, Rosie turned toward the bar and found an empty stool. Sliding onto it, she smiled at Becca's dad. "Hi, Charlie!"

"Rosie!" Charlie stretched across the bar and hugged her. "It's been too long, kiddo! Cherry cola?"

Touched that he still remembered her favorite, she smiled and nodded. He danced to the beat of the music as he made his way toward the soda taps. Along the way, he picked up a glass and filled it with ice.

As he filled the glass with cola, he called out to one of the regulars headed toward the exit, "Have a good one, Ernie!"

The old man waved goodbye on his way outside, and Rosie marveled at Charlie's charm. The man knew everyone in town and treated every person he met like his best friend.

"There you go, little lady." Charlie set the soda in front of Rosie and waved a hand dismissively when she went for her wallet. "Stop that. Your money will never be any good here, Rosie. You know that."

It didn't stop her from trying. She sipped her soda and thanked him.

"How's your father doing? He didn't come in this week." Charlie leaned over the bar. "We're long overdue for some fishing."

Simon frequented both Miller's and the diner in town. He liked to sit and talk with the locals. A close friendship had developed between Charlie and Simon over the years.

"He's good," Rosie said casually. "You know how he is. Always busy with something."

"Charlie, do I need to dance a jig to get a beer over here?" An old man at the end of the bar held up his empty bottle and shook it.

"That's my cue. Take care, sweetie." Charlie gave Rosie a warm smile then made his way toward the old man, striking up a conversation with him.

Rosie's gaze drifted over the people crowded around the bar. A large retail distribution center outside town employed a lot of the locals, and they all seemed to make their way to Miller's after their shifts were done. Some struck up conversations with vacationers—you could spot one from a mile away—and some sat back and glowered at the tourists in poorly concealed irritation. Never mind the fact that tourism kept the town running. The shops on Main Street catered to the vacationers, selling fudge, cheese curds, ice cream, and T-shirts boasting of the great Northwoods.

Cabins dotted the lake edge and the bluffs that towered over the town. The Hart family owned most of them, and Simon invested a lot of the family's revenue back into the town, especially the schools. Most small towns didn't have large indoor swimming pools, state-of-the-art sports venues, and funding for every extracurricular, from art club to drama club to the debate team.

Arms wrapped around Rosie's shoulders from behind, and she jumped at Becca's voice. "All done!"

Turning, she smiled at her friend. "Great! Do you have a ton of homework? I don't want to keep you from it."

"Nah." Becca waved a hand dismissively. "Just need to finish a paper I already started. Besides, I'm starving. So glad I'm not going to be eating alone tonight."

They made their way to the kitchen, and Becca picked up two plates of the chicken special. She must have placed the order for them already. She handed a plate to Rosie, and they went to the outside seating area and found an empty table.

They set their plates down, and Becca darted back into the restaurant and reappeared a few moments later with a soda. Rosie still sipped at the soda she'd gotten from Charlie at the bar. She inhaled deeply through her nose. The chicken smelled amazing. After Becca sat down, they dug into their dinner.

Out on the lake, pontoons glided lazily while speedboats and jet skis buzzed around them like houseflies. The water glowed under the setting sun, and the lights along the boardwalk were starting to blink on. In the distance, an eagle soared over the trees.

"Do you want to go out on the pontoon this weekend? It's supposed to be beautiful out." Becca chewed a mouthful of chicken as she spoke.

Rosie was about to agree, eager for a fun afternoon with her friend, when the memory of her weekend plans hit her. Her shoulders sagged, and her stomach threatened to expel its contents. "I can't. I have something going on this weekend. In fact, I'll be busy every weekend for a while."

"Doing what?" Becca furrowed her brow as she took a drink of her soda.

What should she tell her? Thinking quickly, she blurted, "My father has family friends up near Superior. I'll be going there on the weekends."

"Oookay. Why?"

"It's kind of a long story," Rosie said with a sigh. "I don't really want to talk about it."

Becca eyed Rosie with raised eyebrows for a moment before she shrugged. "Okay. You know you can tell me anything, Rosie."

"I know." Shame heated her cheeks. "Thank you, Becca. You're the best friend I've ever had."

"Bull."

"What?"

"We're good friends, yes." Becca grinned. "But we all know Lucas is your best friend. You guys have gotten so close."

Tucking her hair behind her ear, Rosie glanced at the lake. "We're really good friends."

"Are you sure it isn't more than that? That kiss in the spring—"

"Was just a one-time thing," Rosie said quickly. "We realized our friendship was too important, so we stopped." Guilt washed over her. God, what she wouldn't give to be able to tell Becca every heavenly detail about her relationship with Lucas.

"Yeah, that's what you said over the summer. But there's something different. You light up like a Christmas tree every time he's around."

"You're nuts."

"Am I?"

"Yes." Heat rose from her cheeks to her ears.

"Okay, fine." Becca rolled her eyes. "So, what are we going to do about this whole weekends-away thing?"

"What do you mean?"

"When are you going to make time for your 'best friend'?" Becca made air quotes.

Rosie frowned. "Wednesdays are my afternoons with my grandma. I'll stop here for dinner afterward so we can catch up."

"I guess that will do," Becca said. "I still want to know what's so important that you have to spend every weekend with your dad's family friends. I would say it's weird, but everything about you and your family is weird, so I shouldn't be surprised."

Rosie raised an eyebrow. Her friend didn't know the half of it.

ELEVEN

ROSIE

Saturday morning came too fast. As Rosie opened her eyes, sun streamed through the windows and warmed her face. Sparrows chirped. Normally, the sound filled her with a special kind of happiness, but today, it made her want to scream.

Fighting the urge to bury herself under the covers and never leave her room again, she pushed the blankets back and scooted out of bed. She had plans to take a walk with Lucas before she drove to the Cramers' place.

Dread filled her stomach for what felt like the hundredth time that week. She kept trying to tell herself that it might not be so bad, but then she remembered that awful visit last spring, and it made her want to vomit. William Cramer had talked about her like she was a dog to be bred. And the way he talked about Martha caused a tightening in her chest.

Then there was Bruce Cramer, the horrible man who'd killed her father's cousin Jack. The emotions she'd felt from him were nothing short of malicious hate, and it caused more anxiety in her stomach. How could she spend an entire weekend with them?

She showered quickly and dried her hair then

dressed in a tank top and a pair of jean shorts and hurried down the stairs and out to the patio, where Lucas was waiting for her.

"Ready?"

Rosie nodded, and they walked across the yard and out to the forest. When they were well within the cover of trees, Lucas reached for Rosie's hand. She grasped his tightly as they moved into a clearing. Golden rays of sun streamed through the treetops, casting a glow over the wildflowers that grew in the open patch of tall grass.

As she ran her hand over the yarrow and larkspur, they bloomed in bursts of white and blue and purple. She moved her hand to Lucas's cheek and pushed her body against him, resting her head on his chest. His heartbeat thundered in her ear. Fast. He was nervous.

He rested his hand on her back and kissed the top of her head. "Promise me you'll tell your father immediately if they even look at you wrong."

"I promise."

His breath was warm against her cheek as she looked up into his face.

"I'm sure it will be okay," he said. She knew he was lying, but she smiled anyway.

He kissed her gently, and she moved her hand up to his neck then ran her fingers through the ends of his hair. They held each other close, touching, kissing, and soaking up each precious moment until it was time for her to leave.

"This is silly," Rosie said, brushing a tear from her cheek. "It's just for the weekend."

Holding hands, they walked to the edge of the woods. She sighed as she let go before they stepped out of the forest and into the yard. They crossed the lawn and stepped across the patio and into the house. Her father stood by the patio door, waiting.

"Do you have all you need?" Simon put a hand on her shoulder and steered her through the hallway and into the foyer. Her overnight bag lay on the floor next to the front door where she'd left it last night.

"Yeah. I packed pretty thoroughly."

"I told William I don't want you driving at night. We agreed that you would leave after lunch tomorrow." He smiled. "So really, hardly any time at all. You'll be sleeping most of the time you're there."

Rosie nodded as he picked up her bag and swung it over his shoulder. They stepped onto the veranda and made their way silently down the stone steps to the front walkway. As they crossed the driveway to the garage, Simon placed a hand on her shoulder again. He pulled her into a hug before he put her bag onto the back seat of the Jeep.

"Call me when you get there," Simon whispered as he pulled on one of her curls.

"I will."

"I'm sorry you have to do this, Rosie." He swallowed.

"I know. It's not your fault, Dad."

"Be careful. Call me if anything doesn't feel right. If they're rude or—"

"I will." Rosie smiled and placed a hand on her father's arm. She pushed a calming energy to him. His eyebrows shot to his hairline before he relaxed and smiled. She'd never shared her energy with him before. "I promise."

~

THE JEEP's navigation system guided her north then west. Miles of two-lane highways cut through the forests of Northern Wisconsin. As she drove farther away from home, her stomach sank, and her heart raced. When she finally reached her exit, she thought she might be sick.

She made a few turns, as prompted by the GPS, and took a deep breath as she neared the address. Like Hart House, the Cramers' place had a gated driveway. As she approached, she spotted a figure standing by the gate. The blond head of hair swiveled in her direction, and she immediately recognized the striking green eyes.

Calvin.

She swallowed as she pulled into the driveway and parked in front of the open gate. He gave a little wave then approached the Jeep. She unlocked the door so that he could climb into the passenger seat.

"Hi, Rosie," Calvin said quietly. "My father asked me to come out and meet you. Make sure you didn't get lost."

"Thank you," Rosie answered, her voice clipped and cool. She waited for Calvin to fasten his seat belt before she eased the Jeep forward. The gravel driveway twisted back and forth through the forest, up a steep hill. As they neared the top, the enormous log-cabin-style house came into view.

"Just park in front," Calvin instructed.

"How long were you waiting for me down there?" Rosie realized she was half an hour later than she'd said she would be.

Shrugging, Calvin gave a small smile. "A while. It's all right, though. It's a nice day."

She parked the car by the house, and the front door opened before she climbed out of the Jeep. She fought a groan when William Cramer stepped out to the porch.

"Welcome, Rose!" He descended the steps as she pulled her bag from the back seat and slung it over her shoulder. "We've been so excited for your first visit."

Behind William, Bruce and George exited the house, looking anything but excited. Next, two young boys ran out the door, pushed their way past Bruce and George, and tore down the wood stairs. They slid to a stop in front of Rosie.

"The boys have been especially excited, as you can see." William gestured to the older of the two boys then the younger. "This is Ethan. He's ten. And this is Ian. He's six."

The enthusiasm that emanated from the boys brought a smile to Rosie's face. She nodded to them. "Hello."

"Are you really a girl werewolf? Are you going to marry Calvin?" Ian had a slight lisp, the result of two missing front teeth. It only slightly softened the blow of his words.

Ethan elbowed his little brother and spoke in a loud whisper. "Shut up, Ian."

Calvin's embarrassment thickened the air and made her blush in sympathy.

"Boys, please, go inside." William pointed at the house, and the boys took off, bouncing up the stairs. "Please, come inside, Rose. Let's get you settled in."

The inside of the house looked like something from a vacation-home magazine. The first floor had the living area, kitchen, and another seating area all in one large, open space. An enormous chandelier made of antlers hung above the foyer. Straight ahead, a breakfast bar lined a kitchen with big stainless-steel appliances. To the left, beyond the seating area, floor-to-ceiling windows brightened the room with a spectacular view of the forest below. To the right, in the living room area, an immense stone fireplace filled half the wall.

Beyond the kitchen, a staircase led to a second-floor loft. A wooden railing ran the length of the upper floor, and several doors led to the upstairs rooms. A hallway appeared to lead to more rooms beyond view.

William spoke again. "The help will show you to your room."

A woman suddenly appeared, and Rosie's jaw dropped. The woman couldn't have been much older than twenty, and she wore a maid's uniform that looked like a Halloween costume. The short skirt exposed her fishnet-stocking-clad legs to her upper thighs, and the low, ruffled neckline exposed much more of her chest than Rosie wanted to see. Her blond hair was tied up in a loose bun atop her head, and bright-red lipstick, dark blush, and heavy eye makeup painted her face.

The woman was silent as she stood to the side, waiting patiently for Rosie to follow her. Though her face was impassive, fear and nervousness came off her in waves. With a quick glance at William and Calvin, Rosie stepped forward, and the woman turned and walked toward the stairs. Rosie followed, blushing as she caught a glimpse of the woman's bottom as she jogged up the staircase in front of her.

At the top of the stairs, a hallway led to a row of bedrooms, and the woman stopped at one of the large wooden doors. She turned the knob and stood to the side as she pushed the door open for Rosie.

As Rosie stepped inside, her breath caught in her throat. A four-poster bed filled half the room, covered in pink silk sheets and about a dozen frilly pillows. Across from the bed, a huge television was mounted to the wall. Next to the television, an open door led to a bathroom. Rosie peeked inside at the large vanity and full shower and bath. Then she moved across the floor to a sliding door that led to a balcony. She glanced back at the woman for a second before she opened the door and stepped outside. The view was breathtaking. The house sat atop a large bluff and overlooked a basin. The treetops below were a mixture of crisp green pines and soft oaks and maples that were starting to show signs of autumn colors.

Stepping back into her room, Rosie dropped her bag onto the bed and took another look around. The woman was still standing in the doorway.

"I'm sorry." Rosie cleared her throat. She took a step toward the woman and extended her hand. "I'm Rosie."

The woman stared at Rosie's hand for a moment before flicking her gaze briefly to Rosie's face. She didn't meet Rosie's eyes. Instead, she looked back down at the floor. "Lunch will be served downstairs in the dining room at noon." She actually curtseyed before she turned to leave.

"Wait."

The woman stopped.

"What's your name?"

She turned to Rosie, meeting her eyes for the first time. It was only for a moment, then her gaze quickly turned down again, and her anxiety increased. "I'm Tessa." She curtseyed again before turning and fleeing from the room, closing the door behind her.

TWELVE
ROSIE

Rosie only had about thirty minutes before lunch to unpack, so she sat on the enormous bed and flipped the television on. God only knew what would happen if she didn't show. Part of her wanted to lock the door and stay in her room.

After flipping through the channels for a while, she remembered her promise to call her father, and she fished her phone out of her pocket.

No signal.

Panic flooded her veins. She had been banking on being able to text Lucas all weekend. It was the only thing keeping her from falling off the deep end. Somewhere in the house had to have a signal.

Hesitantly, she opened her door and peeked into the hallway. Holding her phone out in front of her, she moved toward the staircase. Still no signal. She looked over the railing to the first floor. No one was around, so she moved down the stairs, watching her phone along the way. At the base of the stairs, she held her phone out in front of her as she moved toward the sitting area with floor-to-ceiling windows.

Still nothing.

Trying not to cry, she sat down on the corduroy

couch that faced the windows. As she stared out at the forest, some of her anxiety subsided. It was hard not to marvel at the view.

"Did you get settled okay?"

Rosie turned to find Calvin hovering behind her nervously. He was fidgety, clasping his hands together in front of him and pushing his fingers back and forth. He wore a pair of khaki slacks and a button-up shirt under a sweater vest. It looked like a prep school uniform and had Rosie feeling underdressed in her jean shorts and tank top. His blond hair hung in loose waves around his face, and his cheeks reddened slightly under her scrutiny. His eyes matched the evergreens outside.

"Yes, thank you, only..." Rosie held up her phone. "I can't get a signal."

"Oh, yeah." Calvin's mouth twitched in a small smile. "We only get service from one carrier here. If you don't use them, you won't get a signal."

Rosie fought the urge to scream.

"You can use my phone if you need to make a call." Calvin pulled his phone from his pocket and held it out to her.

Standing from the chair, Rosie took the phone. "Thanks. I promised my dad I would let him know when I got here."

She smiled bashfully as she realized she couldn't remember his number. Had she ever actually dialed it? After bringing up his contact information on her own phone, she tapped the number into Calvin's phone. The call went straight to voice mail, and Rosie left him a quick message, explaining she had no service and asking him to call Calvin's phone if he needed to reach her.

"Thank you." Rosie reluctantly handed the phone back to him.

"You're welcome," Calvin said. He stuffed the phone back into his pocket. "Lunch should be ready soon. I can show you to the dining room."

Rosie nodded slowly then followed Calvin past the staircase to a hallway that led to a large dining room. Along the way, he pointed out the fancy billiard room, a bathroom, and a den.

William was already seated as they moved to the table, and Rosie didn't miss the way his eyebrow rose as he ran his gaze over her. He clearly didn't approve of her attire. She would have to remember to pack nicer clothes next weekend, and she ran through what she had in her wardrobe that might be suitable, but then she stopped. Why should she dress up for them? She didn't even want to be there.

Calvin pulled a chair out for her, and she flashed a shy smile and sat. He sat in the seat next to her as Bruce and George filed into the room, each of them taking a seat across from Calvin and Rosie.

The mood in the room darkened, and Rosie's gaze went straight to Bruce. She could feel his distaste from across the table, and he did little to hide it as he sneered at her. No one else seemed to notice, and Rosie quickly averted her gaze, concentrating on the plate in front of her.

Somewhere, an air vent hummed, and Rosie focused on the sound—anything to avoid the awkward stares and the mix of loathing and nervousness in the air. Tessa brought out soup and sandwiches. Her ridiculously short skirt barely covered her backside, and Rosie couldn't suppress the urge to roll her eyes as Bruce stared at the woman as though he were about to eat her, with no shame and no effort to try to hide it. He even reached a hand out to brush his fingers against her thigh at one point.

Finally deciding to break the silence, Rosie cleared her throat. "Where are the boys?"

A huff of air passed through William's lips as he glanced at her. "The boys eat with their nanny in the kitchen. Mealtimes are more peaceful without them."

The energy in the air soured, and Rosie couldn't help feeling as though she'd said something wrong. Her eyes flitted around the room until they met Bruce's glare.

He smiled as he spoke. "Children, much like women, should be seen and not heard."

AFTER LUNCH, Rosie rushed back upstairs, eager to get back to the safety and solitude of her bedroom. She sat on her bed and watched television, desperate to find an entertaining escape from her present situation. She found a selection of movies and chose to watch *Captain America*.

With her spirits lifted, she settled in. All she needed was some popcorn.

A knock on the door squashed her good mood, and she groaned. Maybe she could pretend she was sleeping and didn't hear the knock.

Another knock.

Damn.

"Come in." She didn't feel like getting up. Maybe it was rude, but she didn't care.

The door opened, and Calvin poked his head into the room. The uncertainty and fear that rolled off him set Rosie on edge. "Are you busy?"

Yes. "No." Rosie watched him carefully. "Was there somewhere else I'm supposed to be?"

"No." Calvin smiled. "I just thought you might want some company."

"Oh." Rosie glanced back at the television. "I was just about to watch a movie. You can join me if you'd like."

Calvin nodded as he moved into the room, shutting the door behind him. He sat on the edge of her bed, leaving about two feet between them. His back was ramrod straight, and his hands fidgeted in his lap.

"I have no intention of mating with you." She didn't know why she said it, maybe just to get it out there and make things clear.

Calvin flinched. "I know. This wasn't my idea. My father... Can we just be friends? You're going to be here a lot."

Rosie opened herself up to his energy. It was scared. Timid. Sad. She didn't sense he was there to hurt her. Leaning back against the mountain of pillows on the bed, Rosie started the movie. "Do you like Marvel?"

A small smile ticked at the corner of Calvin's mouth. "I prefer DC, but I like them okay."

"DC? Are you serious? Marvel is way better." Rosie rolled her eyes. "I suppose you're going to say Batman is your favorite superhero?"

"No." Calvin seemed to relax, his smile a little less forced. "Superman."

"Hm. My favorite is Spider-Man. I like the way he moves. And he's always got something witty to say. I'm always stumbling all over my words. I wish I could be more like him."

"I guess that's pretty sound logic," Calvin said. "I just like Superman because he's cool."

They laughed, and Rosie felt herself relax as they watched the movie. When *Captain America* was over, they decided to follow the Marvel Universe timeline and followed it up with *Captain Marvel*.

When Rosie dared to say that Captain Marvel could kick Wonder Woman's ass, Calvin's face screwed up with horror. "What? You're kidding, right? Do you even know what Wonder Woman can do?"

"She's great, but she's not Captain Marvel." Rosie raised an eyebrow. "Just like Batman can't hold a candle to Iron Man."

Calvin's eyes rounded. "Now you're just being stupid."

"Come on!" Rosie laughed. "What can Batman do? Nothing. Iron Man can fly and shoot lasers from his hands. Please. There's no competition."

"Okay, I'll give you that one. Iron Man might be better than Batman. But that's it. I'm still holding my ground on Wonder Woman."

"And..." Rosie grinned. "Captain America is better than Superman."

Closing his eyes, Calvin exhaled. "I thought we could be friends. I was wrong."

The credits rolled for *Captain Marvel*, and Rosie had to admit that she was having fun. It reminded her of her movie marathon nights with Lucas and Sam. They'd had plenty of them over the years. Star Wars, Lord of the Rings, Planet of the Apes, Harry Potter... They'd done them all.

"*Iron Man* next?" Rosie started scrolling through the selection to find another movie.

"It's actually time for supper." Calvin sounded as disappointed as she felt.

"Can't we just skip supper?" Rosie pleaded. "I'm not really hungry."

"I wish we could." Calvin frowned. "My dad would have a fit, though."

"Fine." Rosie stood and turned the television off, and they headed down the stairs together.

As they entered the dining room, a scantily clad Tessa set dinner on the table. Rosie's stomach clenched. Just when she was starting to think the weekends wouldn't be so bad, a reminder of how messed up the whole thing was planted itself front and center.

"You're late," William scolded them as he unfolded his napkin and set it in his lap. Again, he ran his gaze over Rosie's clothes in distaste.

Maybe she would pack something nicer to wear next time, just to avoid those creepy side-eyes.

Holding out Rosie's chair for her, Calvin flitted his gaze to his father quickly as he mumbled an apology.

"Take the crap out of your mouth, and speak clearly," William grumbled.

Calvin straightened. "I'm sorry. We were watching a movie and lost track of time. It won't happen again."

"That's better." William put some meat on his plate then pointed at Rosie. "Now, as for you, I'll have one of the help take your measurements so that we can get you something nice to wear when you're here."

"Excuse me?"

"I don't know how Simon operates things, Rose, but I think you need to learn a little bit about how things are here." A small smile spread across his face, and he pointed his fork at her. "You don't speak unless spoken to. And you always make yourself look nice. Girls are supposed to be pretty and silent." William smirked, and Bruce and George laughed.

Confused, Rosie watched William take a bite and chew it. He winked at her, a grin on his face. Was he joking?

"Dad, she's not a servant. She's a guest." Calvin's voice wavered softly. Rosie almost didn't hear it.

William's smile dropped, and the laughter in his eyes turned to anger so quickly Rosie sucked in a breath. "Are you arguing with me? If you're going to argue, at least argue like a man and not a mouse. That was pathetic."

Calvin shrank into his chair, and William rolled his eyes to the ceiling.

The hurt and fear that emanated from Calvin broke Rosie's heart, and she couldn't help but reach out to him.

As soon as her fingers brushed Calvin's hand, he pushed her away. His chin shook, and his voice hitched when he asked softly, "May I be excused?"

Across the table, Bruce snickered. He mocked Calvin, wiping at imaginary tears and sticking out his lower lip.

"Go, before you start crying like a little baby." William rolled his eyes again and waved a hand.

Calvin stood so abruptly that he almost knocked his chair over. As he rushed from the room, Bruce and George laughed.

Jumping up from the table, Rosie turned to follow him, but William grabbed her arm, his grip tight. She tried to pull away, but his hold tightened even more, eliciting a hiss of pain. "Sit your ass down at the table."

"Let go of my arm."

"I said sit down!"

Rosie shrank back from William, her heart in her throat. This man was crazy. She wanted to tell him to go to hell. She wanted to scratch his eyes out then run like hell, but all she could do was nod. She spent the rest of dinner watching her plate silently until William dismissed her from the table.

THIRTEEN
ROSIE

A KNOCK WOKE ROSIE THE NEXT MORNING. After throwing on a pair of shorts, she slowly opened the door. Tessa stood on the other side, waiting patiently.

"Yes?"

"I'm here to take your measurements."

Coldness settled over her. William was serious about that? She opened the door farther so that Tessa could come in. "I don't think this is necessary. I have plenty of my own clothes. I'll bring something a little more formal next time."

Tessa was quiet as she held out the measuring tape. Rosie sighed and held her arms out to her sides, allowing her to take her measurements.

As Tessa measured her bust, Rosie felt a presence behind her, and a shiver went down her spine.

"Oh good. You're getting your measurements taken." William's voice was upbeat, as though he were commenting on the weather. "I'll have some of the girls do some shopping before you come back."

"Really, that's not necessary. I have my own—"

William furrowed his brow.

Tessa finished up then scurried quickly out of the room, her head down.

"Of course. That's very kind. Thank you."

"I want to apologize for my temper last night, Rose." William moved farther into the room, his gaze going to the window. "Werewolves are a band of brothers. Tradition is important to me. Women have never been more than servants. You're an anomaly."

Rosie's eyes narrowed as she tried not to roll them. When William turned toward her, he furrowed his brow again.

"Don't look at me like that. You'll have to learn, young lady, that this is the way our society is. Your father did you a disservice by raising you to believe anything different. You should be happy. Many were-wolves would love nothing more than to get rid of you. I see your presence as an opportunity to raise a stronger generation of werewolves."

"Is that all I am to you? Breeding stock?" The sting in her sinuses frustrated her. She didn't want to give this jerk the satisfaction of seeing her cry.

"Yes," he said bluntly. His jaw set before he con-tinued. "That's all you are. Get used to it."

"My father agreed to send me on the condition that you treat me—"

"Have I harmed you?" William shrugged and held his hands out in front of him in a placating man-ner. "I've done nothing more than give you a dose of reality. If you go running home to Daddy and cry that you don't want to come back, he'll go to the Council. And what do you think the Council will do to him for disobeying their orders? Don't be fooled by their diplomacy. They're a cruel bunch when they need to be. They'll have no problem eliminating anyone who stands in the way of what's best for our kind."

Rosie stood in front of the floor-to-ceiling windows of the sitting room on the main floor of Cramer House. Birds soared over the treetops, circling the sky. She'd spent most of her morning in a daze. William was right. She couldn't tell her father how horrible Cramer House was. He would go straight to the Council and demand that the visits stop. But he would have no basis for his request. As horrible as they were, the Cramers weren't actually hurting her. And then what? What would the Council do to her father for going against their orders? Because orders or not, if he thought she was in danger, he wouldn't let her visit anymore. He would refuse.

Would they kill him?

She squeezed her eyes shut, the thought causing her to shiver. Her father couldn't protect her from this. But she could protect him from the Council.

The sound of Calvin's laughing caused her to turn. She'd almost forgotten he was sitting on the couch, playing with his phone.

"What are you looking at?" Rosie's mouth quirked. He was really growing on her.

He peeked up at her from behind his phone. "TikTok videos. Wanna see?"

"I want to see, Calvin!" Ian's voice echoed through the room as he ran across the floor, Ethan trailing behind him. "I want to see what's on your phone."

Calvin looked over his shoulder, a concerned crease on his forehead. When he turned back, he smiled at the boys. "Okay. This is a video of—"

"How many times have I told you not to rot the boys' minds with that filth you watch on your phone!"

William made his way down the staircase, an angry scowl on his face.

The boys ran from the room, and Calvin quickly turned off his phone.

"What were you showing them?"

"It was nothing. Just some funny animal videos."

William stopped in front of the sofa. He flitted his gaze to Rosie briefly then shot it back to Calvin. "It's bad enough you watch all that crap. Keep it away from them." He shook his head and walked away, calling over his shoulder, "God knows I don't want them turning out like you."

FOURTEEN
LUCAS

An early-morning run with the pack was exactly what Lucas needed. He'd spent his entire Saturday lifting weights with Michael. If he was going to challenge Marcus, he needed to be stronger. The second he'd asked Michael for help, his friend dropped what he was doing to get started. Michael didn't need much prodding when it came to lifting weights—it was his favorite thing to do, aside from drinking and eating. He didn't seem to care why Lucas wanted to bulk up so badly, but he was eager to help him.

At night, Lucas had lay in bed, thinking about Rosie. He missed her so much. It didn't escape him how pathetic it was that he was moping like a lovesick puppy.

At Sunday breakfast, Simon ordered everyone out for a run. They would hunt their morning meal. Lucas had internally groaned. He didn't want to go out. He wanted to fill his empty stomach with bacon and go back to his room. But as soon as the fresh air hit his bare skin and his body morphed to wolf form, hunting instincts took over, and his bad mood disappeared.

Without Rosie's shock of red fur in the center of the pack, they blended better with the wooded surroundings, and sneaking up on their prey came easily. The doe never saw them coming. They polished her off in less than an hour.

It was while they lay around, licking the blood from their fur, that they heard the voices in the distance.

"That son of a bitch Simon Hart won't let anyone on his land, but I know that red wolf is wandering around here somewhere." Paul Lewis's grating tone was unmistakable, and at his words, a mix of fury and fear ran through Lucas's veins. "I want that pelt. I *will* get that pelt. I'm not letting that asshole stand in my way."

Simon jumped to his feet, his ears perked. The rest of the pack followed suit, ready to do anything their alpha instructed. He raised his nose and sniffed. The obnoxious scent of tobacco and cologne wafted through the air. The same smell...

"Lucas?" Simon asked.

"It's the same smell." The hunter who'd grazed Rosie last spring had had that scent.

"Everyone, stay put." Simon's anger came through his projected voice. *"They're headed in the other direction."*

Wolf hunting season wouldn't start until November, but something told Lucas that wouldn't matter much to Paul Lewis if he spotted them. In the distance, Paul's companion spoke. The voice was unfamiliar.

"You need to be patient, Paul," he said. "We'll see it eventually. I'm telling you. I saw it. You'll see it too."

"Don't know how you get so close with all that

cologne you wear," Paul replied. "You swim in that stuff or what?"

"The deer like it," the man snapped back. "The red wolf must like it too. Got close enough to clip her leg."

"Yeah, well, you leave your gear at my house, and the smell gets everywhere. My whole den smells like your cologne. Take a shower or something."

"Shove it, Lewis," the man said. "Or I won't help you get the wolf."

"Okay. Okay."

Anger boiled in Lucas's veins. The hunter who'd shot Rosie was within his reach. Everything in him wanted to tear his throat out. A low rumble started in his throat, and his lips peeled back, baring his teeth.

"*Settle, Lucas.*" His alpha's voice tamped his temper but only mildly. "*We can't go at them now. We can't kill humans. You know that.*"

"*We have to do something.*" Sam's voice seethed with anger. His hackles rose as he stayed low to the ground. "*They're not supposed to be on our land. We can at least have them arrested.*"

"*And how exactly are we going to prove they were here?*" Michael asked. He positioned himself close to Simon, always ready to protect his alpha. "*I know that smell. It's Paul's hunting buddy. He's been with Paul at Buck's before. Weird guy. Doesn't talk to anyone but Paul. One of those douchebags who always wears sunglasses, even at night. Big, bushy beard and always wearing the same orange hunting beanie.*"

Michael frequented all the local bars. Buck's was just outside town. Popular with the hunting crowd because it had a big parking lot with plenty of room for ATVs and snowmobiles.

"*Keep away from them, Michael,*" Simon said.

"I'll take care of this. I think it's time to run Paul and his family out of town."

~

WHEN ROSIE RETURNED LATER that day from her first weekend away, she put on a wide smile, hugged everyone, and gushed that everything had gone great.

Lucas didn't buy it. Not for one second.

After she disappeared to her room to unpack, he waited. He knew just where she would go when she was done. The old oak tree was like her best friend.

As he stepped quietly through the grass toward her, he could hear her whispered words. She might have been speaking to the tree. She might have been speaking to the squirrels. Hell, maybe she was talking to the grass. He didn't know. Nothing would surprise him.

"Can I join you?"

She didn't seem surprised to see him. Probably heard him coming. Her mop of red curls bobbed in a nod, but she didn't move from her spot.

He lowered himself to the ground and crossed his legs as he scooted close to her. The urge to gather her in his arms and hold her was excruciating, but he fought it, sensing she needed a little space.

"You want to tell me about it?"

She didn't meet his eyes as she shrugged. "There isn't much to tell."

"Come on, Rosie. I know you."

"It was fine." Though she smiled at him, tears pooled in her eyes. "It just sucked being away from home. That's all."

"Did anything happen? Did Calvin—"

"No." She sniffed and rubbed her nose, a small

smile playing at her lips. "Calvin is a pussycat. He wouldn't hurt me."

Jealousy gnawed at him, and he fought to keep his voice even. "You like him."

She nodded. "He was nice to me. We watched movies. I don't think he wants to do this any more than I do."

"Somehow I doubt that." He ground out the words in a low growl.

Her eyebrows shot to her hairline, and an amused smile lit her face. "Are you jealous?"

"Duh."

Musical laughter filled the air, and Lucas gave her a playful shove. His jealous anger dissipated, and a smile quirked his lips.

"So glad my misery brings you joy," he teased. His smile dropped. "Seriously, though. Did you forget why you're there?"

The amusement left her eyes, and Lucas wanted to kick himself and his big mouth.

"Of course I didn't forget. I have no intention of *mating* with him."

"I know." Lucas touched her arm. "I'm sorry."

"Can we talk about something else? What did you do while I was gone?"

"Sat on the porch, waiting for you to return. Like a dog."

Another laugh. The way her face lit up and the gentle way she giggled always filled a hole somewhere deep inside him. He would be perfectly happy spending the rest of his life making her laugh.

After Rosie's weekend with the Cramers, school suddenly didn't seem like such a horrible place. Funny how things could be put into perspective. The dreadful cloud of doom didn't hang over her head as she made her way through the front doors Monday morning. She relished her time with Lucas during first and second period, even while she sat through boring lectures in social studies and American history and tried to ignore the way Cassie undressed Lucas with her eyes.

Predictably, fourth period was the most dreaded part of Rosie's day, but she found it surprisingly easy to ignore Mason as the week progressed. She didn't talk to him unless they were given a lab assignment to complete.

On Thursday, Mason's energy felt particularly anxious and angry as he fidgeted in his seat. He stole glances at her periodically, his anger growing as class dragged on. Finally, when it was time for them to work on their assignment, Mason pinned her with a deadly glare.

"Does your father take pleasure in ruining my father's life?"

The hate behind the hissed words caught her off guard. "What are you talking about?"

"You know exactly what I'm talking about. My dad's account was frozen with the bank, and no one wants to do business with him because of your father and that stupid restraining order."

"Well, maybe your dad shouldn't have set traps on our land."

"He didn't!" Mason looked around the room, then, lowering his voice, he said, "He didn't. It wasn't him. Your dad just has it out for him. It's because of you, isn't it? You asked him to ruin my dad's life because of what happened between us."

"What happened between us?" Rosie couldn't believe what she was hearing. "You mean what you tried to do to me?"

"You're such a lying slut."

"Back off. I'm warning you."

"Or what? Your dad will ruin my life too?"

The ring of the bell startled her, and she quickly gathered her things and shoved them into her backpack. Trying to control the shaking in her hands, she rushed out to the hall and ran directly into Lucas, bouncing off his chest. He grabbed her arms, laughing as he steadied her.

"Whoa, slow down! I finished my trig test a little early, so I figured I'd walk you to lunch." He paused, studying her face. "Rosie? What's wrong?"

The blue in his eyes suddenly turned stormy as he focused on something over her shoulder. She turned to see Mason barreling out of the classroom, straight toward her. As she turned back to Lucas, she could see the pieces clicking into place.

"Leave it, Lucas." She reached for him, but he shook her hand away before she could push her calming energy to him. He stepped forward, placing his body between her and Mason.

"What did you do to her?" His voice was lethal.

The smug smile on Mason's face was a mask. She could feel his nervousness. "What's up, Beckett? Playing bodyguard to your little freak girlfriend again? I'm not going to let you sucker punch me this time."

Pushing between them, Rosie grabbed Lucas's hands. She concentrated on calming him before she turned to Mason. "I told you to back off. I mean it."

"Is there a problem out here?" Mr. McCall stepped out of the classroom and looked from Rosie to Mason then back again.

"No problem." Mason glared at Rosie before he turned to Mr. McCall. "Rosie was just telling me what the assignment was. I forgot to write it down."

～

"I had it under control." Rosie gritted her teeth as she steered the Jeep toward Main Street.

"It didn't look that way."

"He spooked me. That's all." She glanced toward Lucas and sighed at the sad puppy-dog expression on his face. "I appreciate you wanting to take care of me, but you only made it worse."

"I'm sorry. I didn't mean to. It's just..."

"Just what?"

"This whole thing with the Cramers. I can't do anything about it, and it's killing me." He squeezed her hand. "But I *can* do something about Mason. It would make me feel better."

"As much as I would love for you to feel better"— she pulled his hand up to her face and kissed it— "it wouldn't make *me* feel better. Please don't do any-thing to him. I don't want that on my conscience."

"Fine." Lucas rolled his eyes. "You're probably saving me from an ass-beating anyway. Last time, I had Sam backing me up. If I go at the captain of the football team alone, I'm probably asking for a week-long hospital stay."

"I don't know." Rosie squeezed his upper arm. "I think you could hold your own."

She pulled the Jeep into a parking spot by the park and spotted Sam's SUV right away. They'd made plans to meet at Miller's for some cheese curds after school. She jumped out of the driver's side and joined Lucas as they crossed Lake Street.

Inside Miller's, they moved to the corner booth—their regular spot. Rosie held in a snicker when she spotted Becca hanging on the edge of the booth, talking to Sam. She played with her hair with one hand and held the notepad she used to take orders with the other. Her sneaker toed the edge of the bench as she giggled maniacally at something he said.

"Rosie!" She jumped forward and threw her arms around Rosie as they approached the booth.

Giggling at her friend's infectious energy, Rosie hugged her back as Lucas slid into the bench seat across from Sam.

"Sam already put in an order of curds, so they should be up soon," Becca said. "I've got other tables. I'll catch you guys later!"

Becca spun on her heel and skipped across the dining room to one of the few occupied tables. Most of the patrons were at the bar. Three o'clock in the afternoon wasn't exactly the most hoppin' time to be at Miller's, but the regulars didn't care what time it was. A beer and a television were all they needed.

As Rosie slid into the booth next to Lucas, Sam looked at her. "So, are you ready to go back to stay with the pod people again this weekend?" Sam jumped. "Ow! What gives, Beckett?"

"Way to steer clear of that topic, Sam. Didn't we just talk about this? God, you're an idiot." Lucas smacked the side of Sam's head.

Sam swatted back at him, and Rosie laughed, ducking out of the way of their flailing limbs.

"You guys don't have to walk on eggshells around me, you know." She elbowed Lucas. "I'm not going to break."

"See?" Sam stuck his tongue out at Lucas, and Lucas swatted at him again. After he ducked away from Lucas, Sam turned to Rosie again. "Seriously, though. You doing okay?"

Biting her lip, Rosie averted her gaze. Best way to keep the truth from Simon was to keep the truth from *everyone*. "Fine. I'll be fine. Maybe they'll get sick of me and ask me to stop coming, right?" She tucked her hair behind her ear and chuckled.

"Whole thing is messed up," Sam said. "Calvin is a legit freakshow."

Having heard that word tossed in her direction on more than one occasion, Rosie flinched. She barely knew Calvin, but she felt the need to defend him.

"He's not that bad, Sam." She cleared her throat. "It's the adults in that family that give me the heebie-jeebies."

"Not that bad?" Sam shook his head. "It's like there's no one home. Total space cadet."

"He has a lot going on. That's all."

Lucas shifted in his seat as though he was uncomfortable. She glanced his way and caught him scowling at the table.

"Please don't tell me you're becoming a pod person, Rosie," Sam said. "I thought you'd hold out longer. They got to you already? I'm so disappointed!"

"Disappointed about what?" Becca appeared and placed a basket of cheese curds in the middle of the table.

"Nothing," Rosie answered. "We were just talking about the family I'm staying with on the weekends. Sam was just saying how disappointed he'll be that I won't be around. I'm his favorite sister, after all."

Sam rolled his eyes, and Rosie giggled as she reached for a cheese curd.

"You guys crack me up." Becca ruffled Sam's hair then spun on her heel, heading toward the kitchen.

"So, I heard there was a whole thing in the hallway today with Mason." Sam reached for a cheese curd and stuffed it into his mouth.

Rosie ran her hands through her hair. "The gossip in this town is relentless."

"Apparently, he threatened your life, and Lucas pulled a knife on him or something like that."

Rosie rolled her eyes. "And ridiculously exaggerated. Mason was just all upset about this feud between Dad and Paul Lewis."

Sam grinned. "Oh, reeeally? What did he say?"

Rosie raised an eyebrow at his obnoxious smirk. "Something about a frozen account."

Sam laughed. "I went with Dad yesterday. We had a long conversation with the owner of the bank about Paul Lewis. Apparently, Dad and Jim-Bob are like that." Sam crossed his fingers.

"Why?" Rosie knit her brow. "This isn't still about what happened last spring, is it? Because that's no reason to..." She caught Sam and Lucas exchanging glances.

"It's not that, Rosie." Lucas touched her hand under the table. "Paul was hunting on Hart land on Sunday. We were all out for a run and heard him. Your dad has had enough of his trespassing. It's lucky none of us were seen."

Nodding, Rosie gave a tight smile. She tried not to notice how they exchanged glances again.

SIXTEEN
ROSIE

Anxiety burned in Rosie's stomach as she neared the Cramer house for her second weekend visit. Just like last time, Calvin waited for her at the gate and hopped into the Jeep before she steered it up the long driveway.

To her immense relief, no welcoming committee waited on the front porch. As she parked the Jeep, Calvin cleared his throat. Eyes downcast, he spoke softly. "My father asked me to remind you to dress for lunch. He said to check the closet." A scowl formed on Rosie's face, and Calvin frowned. "I'm sorry, Rosie. I really am."

"It's not your fault." Rosie sighed as she grabbed her overnight bag from the back seat and climbed out of the Jeep. She fought the urge to scream as she climbed the steps to the front door. Pompous ass William Cramer. Where did he get off?

Just before she stepped into the house, Calvin called out to her. She turned toward where he still stood in the driveway. He was doing that thing he always did with his hands. The nervous fidgeting. He seemed to be looking everywhere except at Rosie when he spoke.

"Do you think you'd like to continue our movie marathon after lunch today?" He finally looked at her, hope shining in his green eyes.

A smile spread across her face, and her mood lightened. She nodded. How had such a sweet guy managed to be raised in this awful house?

Once inside, she jogged up the stairs, eager to get to the safety of her room before she saw anyone. The door was within sight when Bruce called out to her, his tone scathing.

So close.

She turned to find him leaning in the doorway of what she assumed was his bedroom, cleaning his fingernails with a pocketknife. Gross.

"Back again?" He glanced at her as he spoke. His eyes held such hatred.

"I guess."

"I don't want you here."

Her eyes widened in surprise at his bluntness. "Well, I don't want to be here, so I guess we have something in common."

"We have nothing in common." Bruce straightened and took a step toward her.

Rosie took a step back.

"William wants you here because he thinks you're the answer. The key to a future of full-blooded wolves. I disagree. I think you should never have been born, and to bring more like you into this world is the biggest mistake we can make."

Rosie swallowed as she took another step back. Nothing to say, she turned toward her bedroom door and propelled her way through it. She closed and locked it behind her. Her heart beat frantically. He reminded her so much of Amos. How many werewolves thought like him? And how many thought like William?

She was doomed. She would either be killed or used for breeding. Walls closing in on her, she sank to the floor as her breath hitched. This couldn't be her life. Her future.

Suddenly, she was back in the woods all those years ago after she'd healed Lucas. Her pack—her family—staring at her as though she were a stranger. Amos's words ringing in her ears.

Abomination.

She propped her elbows on her knees and scrubbed her hands over her face, wiping away the tears. She tried to breathe, in through her nose and out through her mouth, through the fear that overwhelmed her.

It took some time, but she finally picked herself up off the floor and moved to the bed. Brooding wasn't going to help anything. If she was late for lunch, it would only make things worse.

She shuffled across the floor to the closet and took a calming breath in through her nose before opening the door. Four garment bags hung neatly inside, each with a Post-it note instructing her on when the garment should be worn. Shoes lined the floor, also labeled with Post-it notes.

Rosie closed her eyes and counted to ten.

She grabbed the garment bag marked Saturday Lunch and placed it on the bed then unzipped it to reveal a pink dress with a light floral pattern and a cardigan. Relief flooded through her. Part of her feared she would find one of the outrageous maid uniforms. This wasn't so bad. Nothing she would normally wear, but it was tasteful.

After dressing, she ran her hands through her hair

and stepped into the hallway. She made her way down the stairs, through the hall, and into the dining room. As she entered, Calvin jumped up from his seat and held her chair out for her. She smiled at him as she sat.

At the head of the table, William watched her closely. The way he ran his eyes up and down her body set her on edge, but she smiled pleasantly. Just get through mealtimes, and the rest would be easy.

Hate soured the air, and she pinpointed the source when she glanced across the table at Bruce. He scowled at her, and Rosie gritted her teeth as she kept the tight smile plastered on her face. Next to Bruce, George looked ready to pass out. Drunk already. It was barely noon.

God, what if the Council ordered her to live here? Could she handle this? No. This couldn't be it. This couldn't be the rest of her life. Living with these people. These awful people.

The sandwich in front of her went untouched as she sat through lunch, counting the minutes until she could go back to her room.

When William finally finished his lunch and dismissed everyone at the table, she rocketed up the stairs. The moment she closed her bedroom door behind her, she ripped the dress off, balled it up, and threw it into the corner. From her overnight bag, she pulled out a pair of sweatpants and the old T-shirt Lucas had let her borrow. She held the shirt to her face and breathed in his scent. Tears pricked her eyes as she slid it over her head. Then she pulled the sweatpants on and climbed onto the enormous bed.

A mound of satiny, lacy pink pillows sat perfectly positioned against the quilted headboard. She grabbed the nearest one and stuffed her face into it to muffle her scream. Once that was out of her system, she leaned back into the mountain of pillows to make herself comfortable while she waited for Calvin. When the knock on the door came, she yelled for him to come in.

His face lit up in a dimpled grin as he entered. "I noticed you didn't eat much at lunch. I brought a snack."

"Oh my God." Rosie sniffed the air. The aroma of buttery popcorn met her nose. "You just became my favorite person."

His smile widened, and he crossed the floor in three long strides. He sat on the edge of the bed and handed her the large bowl. As she dove into the popcorn, she watched him lean back into the pillows, making himself comfortable. It was a change to the stiff posture he maintained through movie time last week. His long legs stretched across the bed, and he crossed one foot over the other. Not as tall as Lucas but above-average height. His blond hair fell loosely around his remarkable green eyes. Definitely handsome in a boyish way. His round cheeks made him look young at first glance, but his eyes held a sadness that aged him.

The movie started, and Rosie set the bowl on the bed between them. They were silent for a while, munching on popcorn and watching the TV.

"I'm willing to admit I was wrong," Calvin said out of the blue.

"Huh?" Rosie popped another kernel into her mouth as she scrunched her face up in confusion.

"Marvel is better than DC."

Rosie giggled as she tossed a piece of popcorn at him. "I told you."

"Hey!" He tossed a piece of popcorn back at her.

"Not all of us are as obsessive about superheroes."

"Oh, it's not just superheroes," Rosie confessed as she crunched on another piece of popcorn. "Movie marathons are big in my house."

"Yeah? What's your favorite?"

Rosie shrugged. "Depends on my mood, I guess. Star Wars, Harry Potter, Lord of the Rings..." Rosie ticked them off on her fingers.

"So, no chick flicks."

Pinning him with a glare, Rosie sighed. "Not all girls fawn over brooding romances."

"Noted."

"Besides, that would never fly with the guys. Any *chick flicks* would be vetoed immediately." Rosie shrugged and turned her attention back to the television.

"You watch a lot of movies together?"

"Yeah. We have a lot of movie nights in the rec room."

"Like...all of you?"

"Sometimes. Other times it's just Daniel, Michael, Sam, Lucas, and me."

Calvin nodded. "My dad said Lucas and Roger were banished from their pack. He thinks your dad should never have taken them in."

"Well, that's the difference between your dad and mine," Rosie snapped. The comment rubbed her the wrong way. "My dad isn't an insensitive prick."

"Whoa, sorry." Calvin raised his hands. "I didn't say I agreed with my father."

"I know," Rosie mumbled. "It's okay. It's just that Roger and Lucas are a part of our pack. I couldn't imagine not having them around."

Calvin furrowed his brow. "You're close?"

"We all are," Rosie said carefully.

"It would be nice to have that." Calvin frowned as he stared at the television.

"Yeah, I guess I can't really picture your family being up for spending quality time together." Rosie laughed nervously. "Do you ever go to a friend's house to hang out? Just to get away from the intensity of this place?"

"I...um." Calvin's cheeks reddened. "I don't really have any friends. Unless you count the ones on TikTok and Instagram."

"I'm sorry."

Calvin shrugged. "Comes with being home-schooled. Not really much of an opportunity to meet other people."

"I guess." An overwhelming sense of loneliness emanated from him, and Rosie felt the need to reach out to him. Instead, she kept her hand glued to her side. "I never really thought about it. That sucks."

Calvin laughed. "Eloquently stated. Yes, it sucks."

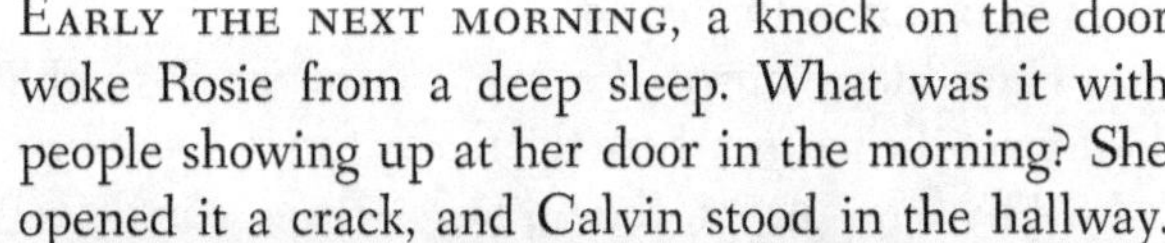

EARLY THE NEXT MORNING, a knock on the door woke Rosie from a deep sleep. What was it with people showing up at her door in the morning? She opened it a crack, and Calvin stood in the hallway. He looked her over and grinned. He pressed his lips together, like he was trying not to laugh.

Rolling her eyes, Rosie ran her hands through her curls. "Laugh it up. You'll have to get used to the morning rat's nest if you're going to wake me up at the butt crack of dawn. What do you want?"

"I thought you might want to go out for a hike. It's a beautiful morning."

God, yes. Getting out of the house? Definitely. Count her in. "Give me a couple of minutes."

She shut the door and used the bathroom then hurried to her duffel bag and rummaged through it until she found a T-shirt and a pair of shorts. After quickly getting dressed, she wrangled her tangles into something resembling a bun then pulled on her tennis shoes and jogged to the door, opened it, and stepped out to join Calvin in the hallway.

"Here." Calvin handed her a muffin. "Figured you'd prefer something mobile over having breakfast at the table with the pack. My dad gave us permission to miss breakfast as long as we're doing something together."

"I knew I liked you." Rosie stuffed a chunk of the blueberry muffin into her mouth as she followed Calvin down the hallway to the stairs.

They headed outside, and Calvin led her down a well-worn path away from the house. A few pines littered the edge of the yard, and they walked through to a trail that went down the side of the bluff. Rosie paused at the head of the trail, which overlooked the basin. Looking down over the treetops, she felt like she was on top of the world.

They hiked down the side of the bluff to the bottom of the basin, where the mossy forest floor burst with life. The plants, the animals—Rosie could feel their energy, and it lifted her spirits. Dozens of species of insects buzzed, and birds sang happily. Plants grew green and lush. Small critters scampered in the brush. A lot were the same species that frequented the forest behind Hart House, yet it all felt new and different.

Rosie sat and took it in. A few chirps and beeps that didn't come from nature pricked her eardrums, and she looked at Calvin. His face was buried in his phone. She rolled her eyes. He seemed to be glued to the thing. And everyone thought *she* was bad.

"What are you looking at now?"

Calvin raised his head, and his cheeks reddened. "It's a TED Talk. Sorry. You seemed like you needed to be alone."

"It's okay." Rosie stood. "We can head back. What's the TED Talk about?"

Calvin shrugged. "I don't know. Something motivational. It always sounds good in theory, but I can never put it into practice."

"I know what you mean. I get tongue-tied around people. Especially the kids at school."

"I'm sure I would if I had kids at a school to get tongue-tied around."

They both laughed.

"Mostly it's just my family." Calvin shrugged again. "I can't talk to them."

"I don't blame you. They're hard to talk to."

They hiked along the bottom of the basin then made their way back up the other side of the bluff. The trip was about three miles long, and Rosie's legs felt like mush in the end. She got plenty of exercise in wolf form but not so much in human form. Mushy legs aside, it was a great morning.

SEVENTEEN
ROSIE

Rosie squinted her left eye as she focused her right one over the microscope. She was supposed to be looking at some kind of cell mitosis, but all she could see were blobs. God, she hated biology.

Mason was useless. He hadn't looked at the slides once, leaving her to fill out the worksheet on her own. She wasn't about to beg for his help. It would do no good anyway. He was engrossed in deep conversation with Jared, another football player and one of Mason's good buddies. Lucky her, Jared sat at the table in front of them, so she got to listen to their enlightened conversations every day.

In the chair directly in front of her, poor Jodi Bernsted was in the same predicament, completing the assignment on her own while Jared ignored her to talk to Mason.

"The Packers are off to a great start this year," Jared whispered. "Did you see the game Sunday? Epic!"

"I missed it," Mason said. "But I'm not sorry. I was with my dad. We went to Rhinelander to look at guns. Picked out a matching set of long-range hunting rifles. Early Christmas presents for both of us."

"Damn! That must have cost a fortune!"

Mason shrugged. "Worth every penny. I can't wait to get my hands on them. We're picking them up in a couple of weeks. Plenty of time to do some target practice before hunting season starts."

"You guys turkey hunting or just deer?"

"No, man, we're wolf hunting."

Rosie dropped her pen. It landed with a clatter and spun across the tabletop. A brick-sized weight settled in her stomach as she watched the pen skitter over the edge of the table. Mason's words echoed in her ears, and her eyes darted in his direction. Mason and Jared stared at her. An unamused frown was etched on Jared's face, but Mason smirked.

"What's up, Hart?" He slid closer. "Don't like that? Got a thing for the cute, fluffy little doggies?"

"She should," Jared said with a snort. "They're her relatives."

Though he'd meant the statement as an insult, Rosie's heart raced at the accuracy of it. Her jaw dropped, but no words came out. Mason moved closer, and his hand snaked down her thigh. In a reflexive jerk, she slapped his grubby paw away and slid her chair back. In her mind, she was back in that room again, pressed up against the wall, looking at the stuffed, mounted wolf while Mason's filthy hands roamed her body.

Her heart leaped to her throat when the bell rang. Everyone in class moved at once, reaching for their things and rushing to the door.

Mason stayed still, holding her captive with his terrifying stare.

Frozen. She couldn't move. She couldn't breathe. That old weight—the one he'd put there months ago—settled on her shoulders, heavier than ever.

"Come on, Lewis!" Jared called out. "I don't want to be stuck in the back of the line at lunch."

Mason chuckled as he finally broke his stare. He grabbed his backpack, swung it over his shoulder, and made his way toward the door.

Feeling crept back into Rosie's limbs, but the heavy weight remained on her shoulders.

~

Rosie stabbed at the slice of cold pizza on her plate. Her stomach rumbled with hunger, but she couldn't bring herself to take a bite. On the other side of the cafeteria, Mason sat huddled with his football buddies. Their laughter drowned out the low hum of chatter in the lunchroom. Her gaze darted to him, and her cheeks heated.

Across the table, Sam buried his face in his food. Next to him, Lucas watched her. She straightened when she caught his gaze, and she forced a smile. His brow crinkled. He wasn't fooled. He knew her too well.

"What is it?"

His projected question didn't surprise her in the least, and she groaned. She really didn't want to talk about it.

"Just a crappy day. I'm fine."

Another round of raucous laughter polluted the air, and Rosie's gaze flitted toward Mason again. When she refocused her attention on Lucas, his expression shifted. He looked angry as he took a bite of his pizza.

"Is he bothering you in class?"

"I told you to leave it alone, Lucas." Rosie's cheeks heated with anger.

"If he's bothering you—"

Rosie slapped her hand on the table. "Stop!"

At Rosie's shout, Sam whipped his head toward her, furrowing his brow with confusion. Lucas frowned, and Rosie immediately regretted her action. An apology was on the tip of her tongue, but before she could form the words, her gaze traveled around the other tables, where dozens of stares pointed in her direction. The walls closed in on her, and the sting in her sinuses warned her of the tears to come. She jumped up from her chair and bolted from the cafeteria.

EIGHTEEN
LUCAS

Echoes in the enormous gymnasium amplified the sounds of dozens of basketballs bouncing and sneakers screeching against the wood floor. Lucas tried to block it all out as he focused on placing one foot in front of the other. The rhythm that came with jogging always put him at ease. He loved to run. Coach Jenkins kept pestering him to join the track team, but organized sports weren't his thing. Being told what to do really wasn't his thing. Running was something he did for himself. Just for himself.

His mind kept replaying what had happened at lunch. Rosie was really upset. He had a pretty good idea what—or who—had caused it. It might have been Lucas she yelled at, but the way she studied Mason— like he'd killed a puppy and made her watch—told him all he needed to know. Asshole must have been giving her a hard time again.

Blood sizzled in his veins. What he wouldn't give to tear that guy's throat out. The wolf inside him thirsted for blood. Except for the barbaric old jerks who hunted women, werewolves didn't kill humans. But Lucas wanted nothing more than to end Mason

Lewis. The enormity of that urge scared him and thrilled him at the same time.

"Beckett!"

Lucas turned. Peter Torgeson jogged up behind him, and Lucas slowed to keep pace with him. They'd been told to run five laps, but he hadn't really been counting.

"You and that Rosie chick are tight." Peter huffed out the words between labored breaths. "She your girlfriend?"

"We're just friends," Lucas snapped. His stomach knotted. Denying Rosie as his mate caused him physical pain. "Why?"

"She's in my biology class fourth period," Peter huffed. He stopped running and bent over, placing his hands on his knees as he tried to catch his breath.

Lucas stopped and turned to Peter, his patience growing thin as the beefy kid heaved.

Peter straightened and took one last deep breath. "Today in class, Mason was totally feeling her up. She looked upset about it. Thought you might want to..."

Lucas didn't wait to hear the rest. A red haze colored his vision as he shot across the gym floor to the double doors that led to the locker room. Mason was in Lucas's gym class, but he spent the time in the weight room. Coach Jenkins didn't want his star athlete to waste time running laps with the peons.

He sprinted to the weight room on the other side. As he burst through the door, he zeroed in on his prey. On the weight bench, Mason held a barbell over his head. The world blurred as Lucas crossed the room and leaped on top of Mason, pushing the barbell into his chest.

"Hey!" Mason's face reddened as Lucas crushed

him under the substantial weight he'd been benching moments before.

"If you ever touch her again, I will end you." The red haze that clouded his vision intensified, and Mason's eyes widened with fear. "I will end you."

"Hey!" Muffled shouts barely pierced his awareness until several hands gripped his arms, pulling him off Mason.

The world came back into full-colored focus as Lucas trembled, panting. As awareness came crashing down on him, he realized how close he'd been to shifting. The wolf inside him begged for Mason's blood, but he pushed the urge down as he stared into Mason's terrified eyes.

Mason's gaze shifted around the room, and he schooled his expression into one of cool indifference. "What the hell, Beckett?"

Someone shoved Lucas. He spun around and shoved back, ready to throw a punch, but his arm was grabbed from behind. He struggled to break free and quickly found himself face-to-face with Coach Jenkins.

"How many times do I have to tell you guys? No fighting in my weight room!" He glared at Lucas. "Get out of here, Beckett! Cool off!"

∾

As Lucas strolled across the parking lot after school, he caught sight of a seething Rosie leaning against the Jeep. Her glare made him want to crawl under the pavement. Damn small towns, small schools, and gossipy teenagers. Word spread fast.

"You couldn't leave it alone?" Rosie's voice shook. "How many times did I ask you to leave it alone?"

"I'm sorry—"

"Save it." Rosie turned and pulled the driver's-side door open, climbed in, then slammed the door shut with more force than necessary.

Lucas huffed out a breath as he rounded the front of the Jeep. He barely had time to climb into the passenger seat before Rosie fired up the engine, hit the gas, and squealed through the parking lot. She pulled the vehicle onto the road and made her way through town. Tears dripped down her cheeks as she focused straight ahead.

Knowing he'd contributed to those tears, Lucas rubbed his hands over his face wearily. He ached to reach out to her, but her posture screamed at him to keep away. "I couldn't help it. I don't know what happened. The wolf took over—"

"Don't give me that, Lucas!" Rosie yelled. "If I gave in to my wolf's every urge, we'd all be in trouble."

"This was different. I've never lost control like that before. You know I wouldn't do anything to hurt you, Rosie."

She blew out a long breath. "I know you wouldn't. And I appreciate you trying to, like, defend my honor or whatever it was you were doing. It's sweet in a demented way."

Lucas couldn't help the laugh that burst forth, but a sharp look from Rosie shut him up.

"Right now, I'm getting pounded over the head with testosterone, and it's making me a little nutty. I have alphas trying to get me to mate with their sons, wolf councils trying to decide my future, and the captain of the football team treating me like crap. The last thing I need is another man trying to exert any control over my life."

"I'm not trying to control you." Lucas scowled. "How could you think that?"

"Um, did I not ask you to drop it? And did you not ignore me and go chasing after Mason like a knuckle-dragging Neanderthal?"

"If someone is hurting you, I'm not just going to sit back and—"

"You will if I ask you to!"

"No, I won't!" Lucas yelled. Rosie flinched, and Lucas sighed. "When it comes to you and your safety, I won't hold back. Not now. Not ever. I'm sorry if you don't like it."

Rosie narrowed her eyes and stared out the window. They spent the rest of the car ride home in silence.

"You'd better watch out! I'm gaining on you!" Rosie pressed the button on the controller to make her kart zoom past Ian's.

On the screen, Ian shot a red shell at Rosie, and her kart spun off the track. He giggled.

"You stinker!" She tossed the controller onto the floor and leaned over to tickle him. He giggled more, falling back against the couch, where Calvin and Ethan sat watching them.

"My turn!" Ethan jumped down to the floor and took the controller from Rosie.

While Ethan and Ian continued to play, Rosie sat on the couch next to Calvin.

He nudged her, and when she looked at him, he laughed. "You're a big kid."

She shrugged. "Maybe. I didn't see you holding back when they asked you to play a few minutes ago."

"Yeah, you play this all the time, though, don't you?" Calvin quirked an eyebrow. "I can tell."

"We play a lot at home." Rosie nodded.

She'd actually been playing a lot more lately. It kept her and Lucas in close proximity but didn't require talking. Things between them were strained.

They'd both carried on like everything was fine, but tension lingered.

No matter how tense things were, they couldn't stay away from each other. Being near him filled a void, eased an ache, and warmed her insides. The fire of her mate bond burned brightly when she was with him, and when she was away, it was like feeling homesick.

September had flown by, and during her dreaded weekend stays with the Cramers, a friendship had blossomed between Calvin and Rosie. Something about him drew her in. Like a lost puppy she wanted to care for. She looked forward to their time together. He almost made the time with the Cramer pack bearable.

Almost.

Sometimes—like today—they played games with the boys. The children's innocence was a welcome change from the heavy weight bearing down on her from the rest of the pack.

"I didn't know girls could play video games." Ian didn't take his eyes from the screen when he spoke. "The nanny doesn't do that."

Ugh. Rosie tried to hold her tongue. The boys' fascination with being in the presence of a female other than their nanny was beyond sad. They all lived such a sheltered life. All they knew was what William decided to spoon-feed them.

Except Calvin. How he'd managed to get away with having a phone with internet baffled her. His window into the real world opened his eyes to things outside the pack house walls. Maybe William didn't fully comprehend what the internet could do or understand the extent of Calvin's internet usage. Maybe he didn't care. Either way, it certainly helped humanize Calvin. Rosie prayed it would be enough to keep him from turning into one of the monsters that made up the rest of the pack.

And Martha said social media wasn't good for anything.

"You want to go watch a movie?" Calvin nudged her again.

"I don't think there's time for a movie before lunch." Rosie stole a glance at her phone. "Maybe Uno?"

"Uno!" Rosie yelled gleefully and giggled as Calvin threw his cards into the air in frustration.

"You beat me every time."

"I think you let me beat you," Rosie said with a laugh.

"I do not let you win." Calvin started gathering the cards.

"You mean you're really that bad at Uno?" Rosie grinned. "That's really sad, Calvin."

"Add it to my list of sad and pathetic life expe-riences."

"Sad, yes. Pathetic, no." Rosie smiled. "You don't give yourself enough credit."

"Credit for what? Not being carted off to live in a looney bin?"

"Well...yeah." Rosie laughed. "For one."

"Hm. Interesting." Calvin stopped shuffling the cards. "What else?"

"You live in the most depressing house in the world with the biggest assholes ever to have walked the earth, but you've still managed to turn out to be a smart, funny, sweet guy."

"Yeah?"

"Yes." Rosie huffed as she impatiently took the cards from Calvin and started shuffling them. "I was surprised the first time you showed me those hilarious TikTok videos. Never would have pegged you for having a crude sense of humor."

Rosie dealt the next hand and smiled, pleased with the grin she'd put on his face. The adoration came off him in waves. She was his only friend, and they'd gotten close. A small inkling of fear nagged at her. What would happen when the visits weren't forced anymore? Would he be hurt if she stopped coming?

A pounding on the door made her jump, and the cards spilled from her hands. Calvin paled, and a frown marred his features. Rosie started to stand, but he held a hand out. He stood and walked to the door then opened it slowly.

William barreled in, knocking Calvin backward into the room. "What the hell is wrong with you?"

Calvin remained silent, studying the carpet. Rosie's stomach somersaulted as she backed across the floor, away from William.

"Bruce told me you've been letting the boys play games on your phone. What have I told you about letting them use your phone?"

"They j-just wanted to know w-what I was playing. I j-just showed them."

"Well, don't!" William yelled. "You're going to turn them into a couple of little brats like you!"

William smiled at Rosie as though he'd just come in for a friendly visit. He turned and strolled out of the room, slamming the door behind him.

Calvin stood, dejected, staring at the closed door. The sadness that poured from him brought tears to her eyes. She wanted to get him out of the hellhole he lived in and take him home with her. Simon would welcome him into the pack.

But then she remembered why she was here in the first place, and her stomach plummeted. As much as she liked Calvin, she had no desire to mate with him, and asking her father to take him in would send the wrong message to the Council, to her father, and to William...

And God only knew how Lucas would react.

As much as she hated it, poor Calvin was on his own.

TWENTY

ROSIE

As a gust of wind blew through the park, hundreds of leaves broke away from high branches and danced in the air. Then the light wind died, and the leaves fluttered down to join the thousands of others that covered the ground. Their crisp edges crunched under Rosie's feet as she strolled through the grass.

She made her way toward Main Street, admiring the picture-perfect scene before her. Storefronts decorated with pumpkins, gourds, and potted mums. Leafy garland wrapped around light posts. Planters situated on street corners, overflowing with fall blooms. Bursts of red, yellow, and orange.

Her weekends away at the Cramers' meant she didn't have as much time to enjoy fall in Hanks Hollow—her favorite time of year, by far. A teacher workday at school meant a day off, and she intended to make the most of it. After a morning of browsing the shops, she headed toward Dave's Diner to join her father and Sam for lunch.

The little restaurant was across from the top of the park, on the corner of Main and Beaumont Streets. Just far enough away from the other side of the park, where Miller's sat on the boardwalk between Lake Street and the water. Each competing restaurant had its own charm. While Miller's provided a beautiful lake view and a supper club atmosphere, the diner was lined with windows that overlooked the park and Main Street. Small-town charm at its best.

The bell over the door jingled a greeting as she stepped inside and scanned the tables for any sign of her father and Sam. A counter and stools lined the area in front of the kitchen, where some of the regulars chatted with Dave, who could be seen flipping burgers at the large stove in the back. Along the windowed walls, the vinyl seats of the booths faded in the sun. Only a few of them were occupied. No sign of Simon or Sam.

"Hey, Rosie!" Dave Owens yelled. "Long time, no see!"

"Shouldn't you be in school, dear?" Carol, Dave's wife, asked as she limped her way up to the host station. The pudgy old woman looked like she needed to sit down. Years of working on her feet had taken a toll on her.

"No school today, Mrs. Owens," Rosie said. "I'm meeting my dad and Sam for lunch."

"Well, sit anywhere, sweetheart." Carol smiled as she handed three menus to Rosie. She shuffled off toward the kitchen, calling over her shoulder, "Do you want some coffee?"

"None for me, but I'm sure Dad will want some." Rosie chose the booth with the best view of the park and slid onto the seat. She placed the menus on the table and turned her father's coffee cup over as Carol walked around the edge of the counter and made her way to Rosie's table with the coffee pot. "I'll take a cherry cola, though. And Sam will have a regular cola."

Steam rose from the coffee that Carol poured into the cup. "What's on the agenda for your day off, dear?"

"I did a little shopping," Rosie said. "Nothing much."

"'Nothing much' sounds like a good day to me. I can't wait for retirement."

"Are you and Mr. Owens thinking about retirement?"

"Oh, honey, we've been thinking about it for years. Finally time for us to do it. We're planning to put this place up for sale next year."

"That will be nice for you, but the town will miss you."

"The town can kiss my big behind. I'm tired." Carol threw her head back and laughed. "I'll get those drinks for you."

"Thank you, Mrs. Owens."

"You betcha, sweetheart." Carol limped back to the kitchen, mumbling something that Rosie couldn't hear. She was a strange woman.

The jingle over the door caught Rosie's attention, and she looked up from her menu. A man stood in the doorway, his gaze frozen in her direction. It appeared he was staring at her, but she couldn't be sure with his dark sunglasses. A full beard covered his face, and an orange stocking cap was pulled low over his head. At first glance, he looked like any other run-of-the-mill local, but something was off. He had a creepy vibe. His energy touched her, and she was taken aback by the hate that flowed from him.

Hate directed at her?

The door opened behind him, and Paul Lewis

walked in, shoving the man. "Don't crowd the doorway. Why don't you get us a table?"

Beanie Man turned toward him. "Let's go somewhere else."

"What?" Paul stared at Beanie Man, then his gaze turned steely as it slid past him to Rosie. "You."

He pointed at Rosie as Beanie Man shoved Paul out of the restaurant. On the sidewalk, they pushed each other a few times before Paul stomped down the sidewalk, Beanie Man traipsing behind him.

Rosie let out a breath. What was that? No one else seemed to have noticed them.

Before she could wrap her head around it, Simon and Sam strolled into the diner. She took a few deep breaths and let the wild beat of her heart calm. Her father had enough trouble with Paul Lewis. He didn't need to hear about this.

"Simon, where the hell have you been?" Dave stepped out of the kitchen and leaned over the counter.

"Hey, Dave! It's been a while! Haven't been to town much." Simon stepped forward and shook Dave's greasy hand. "Sure missed your burgers, though!"

"Well, hell, I'll put one on for you. Extra cheese and onions, right?"

"You know how I like it!"

Dave smiled as he slapped his hand on the counter. "Comin' right up!"

Sam rolled his eyes when he slid into the booth across from Rosie. "Guess the rest of us don't matter."

"Shh! Sam!" Rosie scowled at her brother.

"What? Not like either of them can hear me. They're both deaf."

Rosie nudged him as Mrs. Owens followed Simon to the table, chatting his ear off.

After Simon slid into the seat next to Sam, Mrs. Owens focused her attention on them. "Do you kids know what you want to eat?"

"Burger and fries," they both blurted.

"Good choice," Mrs. Owens said with a wink. She turned and shouted toward the kitchen as she shuffled across the floor. "Dave! Put two more burgers on for the kids!"

The door jingled again, and Rosie's eyes widened as Daniel and Michael strolled in. Both were covered from head to toe in dirt. Simon waved them over, and they made their way across the floor. Daniel slid in next to Rosie, and Michael grabbed a chair and scooted it up to the table. He turned it around and straddled it, resting his arms on the back.

"Thought these two clowns could join us for lunch today," Simon said to Rosie. "Hope you don't mind."

"As long as they leave enough food for the rest of us," Rosie teased. She elbowed Daniel, and he gave her a playful shove.

Mrs. Owens shuffled out of the kitchen and spotted Daniel and Michael. She scowled at Rosie. "You didn't tell me these yahoos were joining you."

"Mrs. Owens." Michael stood from his chair. He turned to the old woman and enveloped her in a hug. "You break my heart."

"Dave!" she yelled as she batted Michael away. "Put four more burgers on. The bottomless pits are here."

"God, you guys are filthy," Rosie said with a laugh.

"Redid the landscaping around one of the cabins." Michael swiped a sip of Rosie's drink. His face puckered. "Ugh. Cherry. Gross, Rosie."

"Serves you right." Rosie took her glass back from Michael's dirty hand.

"Ran into Paul Lewis on the street on the way here," Daniel said. "He gave us a cheerful greeting."

Rosie's heart picked up speed again.

"I'll bet." Sam chuckled.

"I didn't know he knew that many adjectives," Michael said. "Very colorful ones."

"He shouldn't be anywhere near you," Simon snapped. "The restraining order applies to the whole family and all of our properties."

"It's a small town, Simon," Michael said. "I run into him all the time. Just saw him last night again at Buck's."

"He didn't talk to you, did he?" Simon scowled.

"No, he was too busy chatting it up with that weirdo," Michael said.

Simon scowled again and shook his head as though he wanted Michael to shut up, but Michael kept talking.

"Same as usual. Blaze-orange beanie, sunglasses, beard, mouth full of chew, smells like he took a bath in cologne or aftershave or something."

A memory tugged at the corner of Rosie's mind. Tobacco and aftershave...

"Just stay away from them, Michael." Simon rubbed his head as he glared at Michael. "Don't talk to them."

Michael's eyes flitted to Rosie, and his cheeks reddened. "Yessir."

Mrs. Owens brought out the burgers, and Rosie bit her lip while her plate was placed in front of her. The hunter she and Lucas had smelled on their property last spring, when she'd been grazed by a bullet, had smelled like tobacco and aftershave. Lucas had smelled it at the Lewis house later, but maybe Paul Lewis wasn't the one he'd smelled.

A panicked jolt ran through her insides when she realized the grizzled man she'd just seen was the same man who'd shot her. She shivered as his image and the hate he projected burned into her brain.

TWENTY-ONE
LUCAS

"One more, buddy! You can do it!"

Michael's encouragement spurred Lucas forward, and he pushed one more time, pumping the barbell above his head.

Michael quickly grabbed it from him and placed it on the rack. "Nice job! You're making good progress."

Lucas sat up and rubbed his shoulders. "My arms are going to feel like wet noodles tomorrow."

Michael laughed. "Yeah, they will. And they'll hurt too."

"Thanks. That helps."

Slapping him on the back, Michael laughed again. "Anything I can do."

"Seriously, though, thank you." Lucas gestured to the weights.

"Are you kidding me?" Michael tossed a towel at Lucas. "I finally have a workout buddy. I should be thanking you."

A smile tugged at Lucas's lips as he wiped the sweat from his neck.

"Anyway, I need to go hit the shower. I have a date tonight." Michael waggled his eyebrows, slapped

Lucas on the chest, then strolled out of the room, singing at the top of his lungs.

Shaking his head, Lucas made his way out of the weight room and down the hall to his bedroom. He shut the door and peeled his clothes off as he walked to the bathroom. He turned the water on and stepped into the hot stream, letting it fall over his head and wet his hair. His mind strayed to Rosie. They barely talked anymore. Ever since their fight the day he'd attacked Mason.

He knew she was waiting for an apology.

Lucas groaned as he poured shampoo into his hand then scrubbed it into his hair. Why should he apologize? Because he wanted to keep her safe?

Letting the water rinse the shampoo from his hair, he sighed. He'd gone too far. As good as it had felt to lay into Mason, Rosie had asked him not to. He grumbled. Yeah. He definitely needed to apologize for attacking Mason.

But that didn't mean he wouldn't do it again in a heartbeat should the need arise.

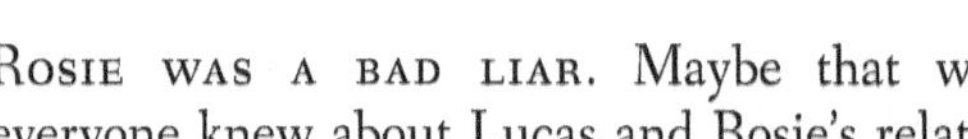

Rosie was a bad liar. Maybe that was why everyone knew about Lucas and Rosie's relationship. Clearly, all the boys knew. They laughed every time Rosie said they were going for a walk.

Now, as Lucas and Rosie sat in the rec room, playing Mario Kart—again—Rosie acted like everything was fine, but it was so clearly not fine. Hadn't been fine for weeks.

Time to eat crow.

Lucas paused the game. When the screen froze,

Rosie shook her controller for a second before she turned to stare at Lucas. She raised an eyebrow.

He forced out, "I'm sorry."

She blinked. "It's fine. Just hit Start."

"No." Lucas laughed. "Not the game. I paused the game on purpose so we could talk."

"Oh." A look of apprehension crossed her face. "Okay."

"I owe you an apology. You asked me not to interfere, and I did anyway. I'm sorry."

Rosie pressed her lips together. "Do you understand why it made me angry?"

Lucas blew out a long breath through his mouth. "Yeah, I get it. Do you get why I didn't listen?"

Rosie frowned. "Yeah. I do."

"Are we good?" God, he hoped so. He missed kissing her so much.

A small smile formed on her lips. "We're good."

"So, do you want to go for a walk?"

Rosie rolled her eyes. "I knew you apologized for a reason. Horny prick." She grinned and leaned back against the couch cushions. "Hit start."

Lucas groaned as he pressed the button.

They played for a few more minutes before Simon walked in, and Lucas paused the game again. Simon rarely came into the rec room. Lucas straightened from his slouched position. Rosie watched Simon as he crossed the floor and sat in the armchair.

"What are you kids playing?" Simon glanced at the television.

Rosie and Lucas exchanged confused looks.

Rosie cleared her throat. "Mario Kart. Everything okay, Dad?"

"Yeah." Simon folded his hands in front of him and

studied his fingers for a moment as though choosing his words carefully. "I just don't get the chance to speak with you much. I want to make sure things are going all right for you with the Cramer visits. You never talk about it."

A dark expression passed over Rosie's face before she forced a smile. "Things are great."

Terrible liar.

Simon scowled. "You would tell me if they weren't?"

She cleared her throat again. "Calvin is really nice to me."

Lucas flinched. It didn't matter that he knew nothing about Calvin. He hated him.

Simon nodded and stood. He stared at Rosie for a moment before turning to leave.

Rosie watched him go then sighed with what looked like relief.

Did she actually think he bought that?

Lucas combed his fingers through Rosie's hair. "You would tell me if things weren't going okay for you there, right?"

Rosie didn't look at him. "There isn't anything I can't handle."

"Rosie?"

She turned to him. "Lucas, if you ever want to go on a walk again, drop it." She smiled. "Press start."

TWENTY-TWO

ROSIE

"Ready or not, here I come!" Rosie yelled as loudly as she could. Somewhere in the trees, Calvin, Ethan, and Ian were hiding.

A giggle floated in the air, followed by Ethan's hushed "Shut up, Ian!"

"You shut up!" came Ian's whispered reply.

"I wonder where everyone is." She raised her voice as she stepped slowly toward the bushes, where she could still hear the hushed arguing.

Unable to resist, she opened herself up, searching for their excited energy. A wave of something else hit her. Adoration...*lust*? She raised her head toward the source of the energy and spotted Calvin crouched on the branch of a tree about ten feet above her.

Surprise flickered across his face as she zeroed in on him. Clearly, he hadn't counted on being found so easily.

Rosie frowned. The energy she'd felt from him left an ache of guilt in her stomach. Was she leading him on? He had to know there couldn't be anything between them.

More giggles came. Rosie spun toward the bushes and leaped forward. "Gotcha!"

The boys screamed and ran. Calvin jumped down from the tree in front of them, eliciting more screams that dissolved into fits of laughter.

"My turn!" Ian shouted. Before anyone could object, he faced the nearest tree and started counting. "One...two...three..."

Grabbing Rosie's hand, Calvin whispered into her ear, "This way."

He tugged her toward another group of bushes. Ethan took off in another direction, frantically searching for a hiding spot.

As they ducked behind some branches, Calvin pulled Rosie closer, and they crouched close to the ground. Their legs brushed together, and Calvin squeezed her hand.

Rosie looked down at his hand then up at his face. Their eyes met, and she saw something in his gaze that made her stomach flip. His energy swept over her, and the guilt tugged harder at her. He leaned forward.

"Stop, Calvin," Rosie whispered, yanking her hand away.

His eyebrows rose, then his brow furrowed. Guilt flooded her as she felt his energy...a mixture of embarrassment and overwhelming disappointment.

"I'm sorry, Calvin," Rosie whispered. "I can't... I mean... I don't feel that way about you. I'm sorry."

"What the hell is this?"

The angry shout made them both jump. A hand reached forward and grabbed Rosie's arm, yanking her out of the bushes. She stumbled in Bruce's vice grip as he shook her. "You little tramp! Can't wait to get him into bed, can you?"

"Bruce! Wait! No!"

Calvin's panicked voice barely registered in

Rosie's brain. Her attention focused on Bruce's furious stare.

"Can't wait to bring the next generation of freak wolf pups into this world? I knew this was a bad idea." Bruce shook her again, and Rosie stumbled to the ground.

"Bruce, don't hurt her!" Ian's cries in the distance formed a lump in Rosie's throat. She turned her head in his direction, and her eyes met Ethan's confused stare. He stood protectively in front of his brother.

"Bruce, what's going on?" Ethan asked.

"Take Ian back to the house, Ethan," Bruce instructed him.

Ethan didn't hesitate. He nodded, turned to Ian, and pulled his brother toward the house. Rosie's heart hammered as she watched them go. She moved to get off the ground, but Bruce's calloused hand pushed her back down.

"Bruce, stop! Leave her alone! We weren't doing anything!" Calvin ran forward, placing himself in front of Rosie.

"Move out of the way, Calvin," Bruce growled. "You're too dumb to know what this wily little trollop is doing to you."

As Bruce took a step toward Rosie, Calvin pushed him back. Surprise flickered across Bruce's face before an angry scowl replaced it. Bruce shoved him hard, and Calvin crashed to the ground next to Rosie.

"Don't you dare push me, you little punk!" Bruce roared.

"What's going on out here?" William's angry shout sliced through the air. He ran out into the yard, his face puckered in anger.

Bruce pinned Calvin and Rosie with an angry glare before he turned to William. "Just a little fight,

William. Calvin here was trying to show off in front of Rose. He shoved me, and I shoved him back."

William's gaze traveled between Bruce and Calvin before settling on Rosie. A small smile spread across his face. "That so? Well, don't let me interrupt."

Beside her, Calvin rose to his feet. He stretched his hand out to help her up.

"No, no. Let her sit and watch," William said.

"What?" Calvin wrinkled his brow.

"I want to see you fight your uncle, Calvin. Maybe having Rose here is the push you needed to get a little taste of manhood. No more scampering around this place like a mouse afraid of his own shadow." William raised his chin. "Come on. Take a swing at Bruce. I want to see it."

Calvin's cheeks reddened as he glanced from his father to Bruce. He took a step back, and his gaze slid to the ground.

With a disappointed sigh, William shook his head. "That's what I thought. You'll always be a mouse, kid."

~

A TENSE SILENCE lingered in the air that night. Calvin sat on the floor in Rosie's room, his back leaned against the bed. Tears wet his cheeks while they watched a movie.

When she couldn't take his silence anymore, Rosie said softly, "I'm sorry, Calvin. I like you a lot. As a friend. A good friend. I don't want to hurt our friendship—"

"Just forget about it." Calvin shook his head. "I was stupid to think you would want me."

"That's not it." Rosie huffed. "I just—"

"Whatever. It's okay." Calvin sniffed. "I'm sorry. I shouldn't have tried to kiss you."

Rosie sighed. "How did you manage to turn out to be such a nice guy after being raised in this house?"

A hiccupped sob was her only answer at first, then Calvin's angry words surprised her. "You mean how did I become such a pansy?"

"No. That's not what I meant at all." Rosie bit her lip and tentatively reached a hand out toward him. Resting her fingers on his shoulder, she closed her eyes and let her calming energy pass to him.

When she opened her eyes, he was staring at her, his mouth gaping.

"It's just something I've always been able to do. Probably better not say anything to your family. They might burn me at the stake."

"A nanny."

"What?"

"You asked what makes me so different from the rest of them. I had a nanny when I was young. She was good to me. She raised me from the time I was a baby until I was around eight years old. We spent every moment together, playing games, and she taught me to read and helped me with my homework. She was as close to a mother as you could get. My father said she was too gentle with me. She argued with him and told him to let me be a kid.

"At first, he seemed to let it go. After a while, he started complaining that I was getting too soft. Too whiny. He blamed her for everything. Yelled at her all the time. One day, I cried and begged him to leave her alone." A fresh round of tears sprang from his eyes as he scrunched his face up in agony. "That night, he took the nanny and me out to the woods. He left us in a clearing, then he shifted. The rest of the pack showed up, and they circled us. They kept lashing out, biting at her. I can still hear her screams. I can still smell her fear. They killed her slowly, right in front of me."

TWENTY-THREE
ROSIE

TRADITIONALLY, SATURDAY NIGHTS HAD ALWAYS been reserved for hanging out. Rosie, Sam, and Lucas played board games or video games then followed them with a run in the woods. Even as they got older and Sam started dating a new girl every week, they reserved their Saturday nights for one another. It wasn't even something they planned. They just always seemed to congregate in the rec room and decide what they were doing from there. Sometimes they headed into town to listen to music in the park or wander around the downtown area. Usually, they stayed in and found something to do.

When Rosie had started spending her weekends with the Cramers, she worried their weekly hangouts would end, or Lucas and Sam would carry on without her. She was pleased when they started congregating in the rec room on Sunday nights instead.

Tonight, they had somehow decided to build a puzzle. Mario Kart must have been getting old. Sam and Lucas probably played it nonstop while she was gone. But as much as she loved a good puzzle, she couldn't get into it. Her mind was still with Calvin and the haunting conversation she'd had with him.

"Rosie!" Sam's sharp hiss startled her as he snatched a puzzle piece from her hand. "Have you seriously been holding on to this? I said I was looking for a corner piece with a feather on it like three times."

Whoops. She'd been holding that piece for a long time. "Sorry, Sammy."

"What's got you all spacey tonight, anyway?" Sam's mood brightened as he clicked the missing piece into place. "You look like you're a million miles away."

"Nothing."

She didn't want to repeat what Calvin had said. It haunted her, weighing her down like a heavy blanket. The cruelty and hate she'd witnessed in the past month and a half depressed her. Was this what the world was like outside the Hart pack? Had she been sheltered that much in her life?

The question sat on the edge of her tongue, and she finally let it pass into the open. "Do you think the rest of the werewolf world is like the Cramers? Are they all that horrible?"

Sam raised an eyebrow, but he didn't look at Rosie. He opened his mouth, like he was going to say something, but he closed it again.

"No," Lucas chimed in.

Some of the weight eased from her shoulders. She hadn't realized how much she needed to hear it. "If they were, my dad would be like that, and he's not."

"And neither is the rest of the Beckett pack," he added. *"Remember, I know them. They're not like that, Rosie. Not at all."*

Warmth spread through her. The words were exactly what she needed to hear.

"The Cramers are crazy," Sam said finally. "They

sit in their house, cut off from the outside world, homeschooling their kids. Hell, I doubt they ever leave."

It was true. She hadn't seen anyone leave once in the time she'd been there.

"That's it." Sam clicked the final puzzle piece into place. "Who's up for a run?"

~

Cool fall nights would always be Rosie's favorite time to run. Leaves changed from green to scarlet and gold, and everything felt crisp. The smell of campfires off in the distance mingled with the smell of the dead leaves that crunched under her paws. A silvery glow from the moon lit the sky, brightening the slivers of clouds that hung around it.

Sam's howl echoed through the trees, and Rosie pumped her legs faster as she tried to keep up with the boys. They were bigger, their legs more powerful. Seemed like she was always falling behind.

"I call dibs on first at hunter!" Sam's voice echoed in her head, and she huffed something that resembled a laugh through her snout. They were old enough to hunt real prey, but the boys still liked to play games. They'd been playing hunters and prey—the wolf version of hide and seek—since they were pups.

"You were hunter last time," Lucas called out. *"It took you so long to find us, Rosie and I never got a turn."*

"Fine! One of you be hunter, then."

Lucas's voice filled her head before she had the chance to speak. *"You're up, Rosie! I'll be hunter next time."*

"Ha! You'll get the chance tonight. Unlike some wolves, it won't take me all night to find you!"

Silence met her challenge, and Rosie skidded to a halt, cocking her head and perking her ears. The forest grew quiet. The game was on.

Pressing her nose to the ground, she took a big whiff. The woodsy scent of leaves and bark overwhelmed her senses, and she moved in a zigzag pattern, trying to sniff out one of the boys.

Leaves...leaves...a mouse... Rosie kept her nose to the dirt as she moved back and forth through trees, stopping to check out shrubs, and darting this way and that. Finally, a new smell hit her. Dirty, oily fur. Bingo.

She followed the scent to the right. The oily stench grew stronger.

"You guys need to shower more. You reek!" She projected a teasing laugh as she zeroed in on a patch of long grass where the stench was stronger. Just as the smell got even more potent—almost enough for her to distinguish which of the boys was hiding there —the smell of skunk from somewhere nearby hit her.

"Ugh!" She shook her head, fighting the urge to gag.

She focused on the thick blades and could just barely make out a shape. *"Found you! Show yourself."*

The shape in the grass stayed still, and she blew out a breath through her wet nose. *"Come on. I found you. Don't make me come in there."*

Something brought an uneasy tension to her stomach, and her hackles rose. She bared her teeth as the air around her grew thick. Cautiously, she opened herself up, searching the energy of the living things around her. What she felt made her recoil.

Malice. Hate.

Slowly, the shape emerged from the grass. She could barely make out the pitch-black fur, even with her keen wolf senses. Michael and Stuart both had black fur, but they had white patches on their chests. Only Amos's coat was completely black.

"*Amos?*"

His lip curled as a low growl rumbled in his throat. With his eyes narrowed, he bared his sharp fangs. Werewolves often growled at one another to convey annoyance or a warning. His growl was neither. This was malicious. The type of growl that came just before an attack but worse. Hate emanated from him in a way she'd never felt before. Amos had always hated her but this...

Rosie backed up slowly. Her voice shook. "*Amos?*"

"*Rosie?*" Lucas's voice came from behind her, and she turned toward him as he crashed through the trees. She whipped her head back toward Amos, but the grassy patch where he had been standing was empty.

"*He was here...*" Rosie straightened and sniffed the air. The stench of skunk hit her again, and she winced.

"*Who?*" Lucas took a step toward her, his head low. "*You got quiet. I was getting worried.*"

"*Amos. He was here just a second ago.*"

"*I thought it wouldn't take you all night to find us.*" Sam mocked her as he sprinted toward them from the north. "*All talk...*"

"*Shh!*"

Sam's ears went back, and he ducked to the ground at her hissed warning. He twitched his ears, listening, before he asked, "*What's going on?*"

Rosie stilled. The forest was too quiet. No frogs

chirped, no owls screeched, no racoons made noise, and no mice skittered through the underbrush. She sighed. *"Amos was here. He was growling at me."*

Sam stepped forward and sniffed the grass then flinched. *"Are you sure? All I smell is skunk. I don't hear anything. Maybe it was a shadow."*

"I thought I saw him. I could have sworn..." Rosie huffed. *"Can we go home?"*

After a moment of awkward silence while Sam and Lucas exchanged glances, Lucas said quietly, *"Sure, Rosie. We can go home."*

No one spoke as they made their way back to the house. In the yard, Rosie used her sharp teeth to pick up her clothes, trying not to slobber all over them, and trotted behind a tall bush. There, she shifted to human form. She pulled her T-shirt over her head and shimmied into her jeans before joining the boys back out on the lawn.

Together, they shuffled through the grass and over the patio to the sliding glass door. As she reached for the handle, Rosie glanced through the window and froze. She could see some of the pack sitting at the ta-ble, in the midst of a card game. The half-empty drinks and their rumpled clothes indicated they'd been there awhile. Her father, Stuart...

And Amos.

As the end of October neared, talk of deer hunting season began at school. September and October made up bow hunting season, but most of the area hunters used guns. Deer couldn't be hunted with firearms until late November. Also in November, open season on wolves would begin.

The hallways at school buzzed with excitement over plans for upcoming hunting trips. Every year, the school shut down the entire week of Thanksgiving when gun season opened. Since two-thirds of the students and many of the teachers went out deer hunting, holding classes was pointless. The time was made up at the end of the year.

In Hanks Hollow, venison was a staple of the local diet. It topped the menu in every restaurant, and the shelves of the local meat market overflowed with sausage, steak, and brats. The town had a taxidermist and an enormous butcher shop that took in new kills for processing on Mondays. The Monday after opening weekend started with a long line of pickup trucks carrying deer carcasses in their truck beds. Trophies of a successful weekend.

Hunting season added a new element of stress for

the pack, especially for Simon. He was continually hounded with requests to hunt on their property. Keeping the hunters away was like keeping ants away from spilled food. They just kept coming. Hunters on their property made their wolf runs more dangerous.

"My father's hunting buddy said he spotted the red wolf again."

Mason's words caused a spike of pain in Rosie's brain. She hadn't forgotten about what he had said to her at the party in the spring. Their prized wolf harvest was mounted to a stand, and Mason had delighted in telling her all about how they planned to kill another. He'd told her about the red wolf his father was determined to hunt down and make part of his collection. She'd never told anyone what he said. Not even Lucas.

"My dad promised we're going to get it this year. It'll make a freaking badass rug."

She felt lightheaded as she pictured her own pelt lying on the floor in front of the fireplace. Of course, that would never happen. Werewolves shifted to their human forms when they died.

Rosie was the only red wolf in the area. How had she been seen? It had to mean that Beanie Man was trespassing on their property again. Why would he be wandering so close to their home? She hadn't gone out past the ravine.

If she told her father what Mason had said, she would be locked up tighter than Al Capone in Alcatraz. The idea of being kept from going out running caused a tingle of fear down her spine. To run with the pack, especially on a full moon, was the most driving innate desire of any wolf.

As the whispered conversation between Mason and Jared continued, Rosie's head began to pound, and her stomach tightened. When she didn't think she could take any more, she growled impatiently and glared. "Would you two shut up already?"

Conversation ceased, and they both stared at her. Mason leaned forward, and she scooted her chair back. As he inched his hand toward her, heat rose up her neck to her cheeks. She slapped his hand away, and he laughed.

"What's with you, Hart?"

"You're a jerk. You know the wolf population is dwindling, right? Extinction is a thing."

"Wolves are filthy varmints. We're going to wipe them all from the map, then we're going to make them into rugs. Maybe I'll bring one to you. Put it on your front lawn."

"You're a pig."

"Yeah, but you like that, don't you." He leaned closer, inches from her face. "I know you want me. I see how you watch me."

Nausea roiled in her stomach, and she balled her hands into fists. "Get over yourself."

Mason shrugged and leaned back. His cocky grin didn't leave his face, and he winked at her. Next to him, Jared laughed.

She shifted her stare to the clock, silently urging the time to go faster.

"Ugh. He's such an ass. Just forget him." Becca wrinkled her nose as she pinned a leafy wreath to the wall above the rows of top-shelf liquor. "He's just trying to get a rise out of you."

"I know," Rosie mumbled.

"Hand me that garland."

Rosie slid off the bar stool and reached for the balled-up leaf garland on top of the polished wood bar. She'd agreed to help Becca decorate Miller's with some festive fall foliage, and the restaurant was starting to look like an Instagram post.

Vases of sunflowers sat atop each table in the dining room, adding pops of bright yellow among the rustic outdoorsy decor. An enormous mounted deer head that served as a focal point on the back wall was decorated with a headpiece of fall blossoms and autumn colors that wound around its antlers in an intricate display. Leafy garland and stringed lights adorned all the doorways and the edge of the bar top.

"Do you think it's too much?" Becca scrunched her face as Rosie rounded the end of the bar and handed her the garland. "I go overboard sometimes."

"I think it's perfect. You're good at this."

Becca had that special touch and made everything look amazing. In addition to being one of those people who rolled out of bed looking like a model, she was just good at making lemons into lemonade. How many times had she tamed Rosie's frizzy hot mess of hair into some beautiful updo that Rosie could never dream of crafting on her own?

"Thanks, sweetie." Becca strung the last of the garland above the bar. "I think that will do it."

"I guess I'd better head home." Rosie sighed. "I have homework."

"Thank you for your help," Becca said as she stepped off the ladder. "Hey, before I forget, you want to go costume shopping next week?"

"Costume shopping?"

"Yeah. If we don't go soon, all the good costumes will be gone, and we'll have to drive a half hour to find something."

"I'm not going trick-or-treating. I think I outgrew that a few years ago." Rosie rolled her eyes.

"No, dummy. The town party. Last year, you promised you would dress up with me this year."

Hanks Hollow had a Halloween bash every year in the square. From mid-September until Thanksgiving, the park exploded with fall decor—haybales, lights, mums, marigolds, pumpkins. The town went all out, and vacationers ate it up. The Halloween bash was legendary. People dressed in costumes, and they had carnival games, cider, caramel apples, music, campfires, and a haunted maze.

When Rosie and Becca were young, they'd looked forward to the bash every year. They coordinated costumes and spent the entire day playing games and getting sick on candy and snacks. As they grew older, it became less appealing, and eventually, they stopped going. Last year, in a fit of nostalgia, Becca had made Rosie promise to go this year.

"You're seriously holding me to a promise I made a year ago?"

"Hell yeah, I am. What do you say? The costume shop just opened up last week."

A storefront on Main Street served as a seasonal spot. It sold costumes and fall decorations in autumn, Christmas decorations around the holidays and bathing suits and souvenirs in the summer.

"Fine. What did you have in mind?"

"Witches."

Rosie sucked in a breath. "What?"

"We're going as witches. Like from *Wicked*. One of us can be the good witch, and one of us can be the bad witch. What do you think?"

"I think you'll make me wear green makeup, and I don't want to wear green makeup."

"Fine. We can both be the good witch. Come on. Please? It will be fun." Becca clasped her hands.

Rosie finally relented. "Okay, okay. It does sort of sound like fun."

"Yes! Thank you, Rosie! This will be so great!" Becca gave a sly smile. "Maybe you can ask Lucas to dress up as your Wizard of Oz."

Rosie sighed. "This again?"

"Oh, come on. You guys are so obviously in love. Can you just stop with the pretending?"

"Good night, Becca."

Rosie's heart raced. Maybe she and Lucas weren't doing such a great job of hiding their relationship after all. Who else knew about them?

TWENTY-FIVE
LUCAS

Lucas leaned back into the couch cushions and mindlessly pressed the buttons on the video game controller, only half paying attention to what was happening on screen. He kept watching Rosie. She sat on the floor, her math homework spread out on the coffee table, chewing on the end of a pencil while she rested her forehead against the arm she had propped on top of her books.

She'd been stuck on the same problem for five minutes. It took every ounce of restraint Lucas had not to grab the pencil from her and write down the answer.

On the other side of the rec room, Sam, Daniel, Michael, and Stuart played cards at the game table. Any moment now, Simon would come in and yell at Sam for playing games instead of doing homework.

"Ugh." Rosie slammed her pencil down. "I hate math."

All eyes turned to her, and her face reddened.

Stuart stood from the game table and shuffled across the floor. Rosie eyed him warily.

"I can help you. I used to be pretty good at math."

Rosie studied Stuart's face. Raw emotion glistened in her eyes before she narrowed her gaze and furrowed her brow. She gathered her papers and stuffed them into her backpack. "I've had enough studying."

Standing, she tossed her backpack onto the couch and sat down next to Lucas. She pulled out her phone, pointedly ignoring Stuart, and started scrolling through TikTok.

The sadness on Stuart's old, wrinkled face made Lucas's chest tighten. Rosie had barely spoken to him over the summer, and everyone could see how it hurt him. Not that Lucas blamed her. What Start had done was horrifying. Still...

"Hey, Stuart, you playing or what?" Sam called from the card table.

Lucas met Sam's stare. Daniel and Michael frowned. They'd all seen the exchange, but the rest of them didn't know the reason behind her coldness. Rosie had shared it with Lucas and made him swear not to tell anyone. Sam's expression questioned Lucas. *What the hell was that?*

Lucas shrugged.

Rosie huffed as she dragged her headphones out of her backpack and put them over her ears.

Not bothering to answer Sam, Stuart lowered his head and shuffled out of the room, almost bumping into Simon as he strolled in.

Simon placed his hands on his hips as his eyes bored into Sam. "Samuel, why are you playing games instead of doing your homework?"

~

A COOL EVENING breeze rustled the leaves of the giant oak tree Lucas and Rosie were leaning on, and he felt her shiver. He sighed. She wore a short-sleeved shirt, and goose bumps covered her skin.

He shook himself out of his flannel. The tee he wore underneath was one of his favorites—a gift from Shawn—and it was starting to thin from being worn so often. His uncle had gotten the Nirvana shirt from one of their concerts in the nineties. Now he would be cold, but better him than Rosie. "Where is your coat?"

"You're not wearing one either," Rosie groused as he draped his flannel over her shoulders. She tried to refuse, pushing it toward him, but he swatted her hand away and draped it over her shoulders again. "Now you'll be cold."

"I've got your love to keep me warm."

Her lips ticked up in a small smile. "Isn't that a song?"

"Yeah. An old one."

"Sing it to me?"

"Very funny."

She pouted, and he studied the freckles that popped against her pale skin.

"That's not going to work on me."

"Hm."

She shivered again, and he cursed under his breath. He pulled her toward him, wrapping his arm around her back. She tucked her head under his chin, and her soft hair tickled his face. So soft. Like silk. He ran a hand through the strands, winding the curls around his fingers.

In the distance, an owl hooted. Lucas looked toward the sound, and his keen vision caught sight of the bird perched on a branch a few dozen yards away.

"Lucas?"

"Yeah?"

"I talked to Becca today. She knows something is going on with us. I think we need to be more careful."

"I don't know how much more careful we can be." Being careful was killing him. He hated ignoring the urge to reach out for her every hour of every day. He counted the minutes until they could be alone together again. She was the oxygen that fed the fire inside him. Without her, the flames dwindled and left him feeling cold.

"I'm afraid."

Lucas tightened his hold on her. "What are you afraid of?"

"I'm afraid the Council will find out about us and take you away from me."

"Nothing could keep me from you." Lucas closed his eyes as she ran her hand up his arm. The electric pleasure of her touch was intoxicating. He kissed the top of her head and breathed in the lavender aroma mixed with sweet-smelling shampoo that was Rosie.

She tilted her head back, and her red-brown eyes bored into his. His gaze trailed down to her lips, and the urge overtook him. He captured her mouth with his. She tasted sweet. Had she been eating chocolate? It mixed with her lip balm and tasted like cherry cordial.

Her lips parted, inviting him in, and he accepted. Heat flooded through him as his body reacted, and his wolf screamed at him to claim her. He ran his hands over her face, her hair, down her arms. The urge intensified, and he pulled away before it became more than he could control.

Stopping was getting harder and harder to do.

"We should head back," he muttered.

Her shoulders slumped with disappointment. "I guess."

Neither of them moved.

"I have to tell you something." Rosie picked at her fingernails, avoiding his gaze.

"Okay."

She cleared her throat. "Nothing happened..."

Lucas tensed. The inflection in her voice told him otherwise. He wasn't going to like what was coming.

"It was just a misunderstanding. Calvin understands that there can't be anything between us now, so it won't happen again."

Damn. He really, really hated Calvin. "What won't happen?"

"He...well... He tried to kiss me. But I stopped him, and nothing happened."

Anger grew hot, and the flames of his mate bond roared. Lucas dug his nails into his palm and tried to tamp it down. This territorial hold he felt for her was exhausting. Seriously, when did he go all caveman?

"Lucas, stop it." Rosie furrowed her brow. "I told you nothing happened. I stopped it before it started. We understand each other now. It's done."

Lucas raised his shoulders. "I didn't say anything!"

"Yeah, but you're scowling." Rosie studied him. "It's a cute scowl, but it's not necessary. Nothing will happen with Calvin. I promise."

Lucas nodded. In his head, he was picturing himself sinking his wolf teeth into Calvin's throat. "Okay."

Rosie sighed. "Okay. If it makes you feel better, I kind of have a little of that territorial thing going on too. I have to restrain myself every time another girl ogles you."

"No one ogles me."

"Ha!" Rosie's voice went high. "Are you that

oblivious? Lucas, girls stare at you all the time with their ugly, stupid eyes. Have you seen cake-face Cassie? She stares at you constantly. Stupid slut."

Lucas grinned. One of the great things about Rosie? She didn't hold back.

TWENTY-SIX
ROSIE

CALVIN EYED THE BACK OF ROSIE'S JEEP WITH A wrinkled nose. "What do you want to do with these?"

"Carve them, of course." Rosie sighed. "Haven't you guys ever carved pumpkins before?"

"Um. No?"

God, their life was sad. "Well, you're going to today. I have enough for us and the boys. I thought they would like it."

"I'm sure they will." Calvin looked down at the ground and kicked a stone. "About last weekend. I'm sorry, Rosie. I shouldn't have tried to kiss you. I've never been around a girl before, you know? I don't want this to ruin our friendship."

"You don't need to apologize, Calvin." He peeked at her bashfully from under his curtain of blond hair when she placed a hand on his arm. "There was nothing wrong with what you did. Don't be afraid to do that with other girls. And trust me—you didn't ruin our friendship. Our friendship is rock solid."

Calvin's mouth quirked in a small smile as he hefted two of the pumpkins from the back of the Jeep. "Thankfully, my father isn't here. Fun isn't in his vocabulary. I don't think he would like this."

"He really is a wet blanket, isn't he?" Rosie lifted one of the other pumpkins out of the Jeep. She eyed the other and hummed. She didn't have that whole upper body strength thing going for her. "I think we'll have to make two trips."

Calvin laughed. "Wimp."

A surprised laugh bubbled from her throat, and she kicked, catching him in the leg.

They made their way up the wooden stairs to the front door. Calvin set one of the pumpkins down and opened the door, and Rosie stepped through. They carried the pumpkins to the breakfast bar and set them down on the granite surface.

"It's going to get messy. I should have brought a plastic tablecloth." Rosie's gaze roamed over the pristine kitchen. Like Hart House, the Cramer house had more than one. One was for "casual" use by the werewolves, and the other was where the human servants did all the meal preparation.

"It'll be fine. Tessa will clean it up."

"Or...we can clean up after ourselves." Rosie gave him a dirty look. If she made a deliberate mess and insisted on Martha cleaning up after her, she would get it from both Martha and her dad.

"Yeah, sorry." Calvin blushed before he headed back toward the door. "I'll go get the other pumpkin. I think the boys are in their playroom."

Rosie went upstairs and shuffled down to the end of the hall, where the boys had a giant playroom. She knocked on the open door as she poked her head in. The boys were on the floor, in the middle of a sea of Lego bricks.

"Hey, guys."

"Rosie!" Ian jumped up, ran to Rosie's side, and threw his arms around her waist.

She hugged him back and nodded to Ethan, who stayed planted on the floor. He gave her a small smile in return.

"I brought something for us to do this afternoon," Rosie said.

"We're already doing something," Ethan grumbled.

"What is it? What is it?" Ian jumped up and down. His excitement was infectious, and Rosie's spirits lifted.

"I brought pumpkins for us to carve."

The blank looks she received from both boys broke her heart a little.

"It's something you do for Halloween."

"Yeah." Ethan shrugged. "I've seen it on TV before. Doesn't look like much fun."

"Well, it is fun, and we're going to do it."

"Yay! Let's go!" Ian took off down the hall, toward the stairs.

Ethan stayed rooted to the floor, and Rosie frowned. "Please, Ethan? Will you give it a try?"

After a huff, Ethan said, "Fine," then stood and tiptoed through the Lego bricks toward her.

As Rosie watched him walk unenthusiastically down the hall, she frowned again. Ian still had that childlike innocence, but Ethan's childhood was getting robbed from him. He was already spiraling into acceptance of the mundane existence their life provided. He was becoming a Cramer.

As it turned out, pumpkin carving brought out the child in everyone, including Calvin. After they spread out and drew pictures of the faces they wanted to carve, they proceeded to cut off the tops of the pumpkins and scoop out the guts. Rosie was helping Ian draw a face on his pumpkin when a slimy, wet mass slapped her cheek.

"Ugh, what the..." She wiped the goo from her face, and her eyes darted to the other side of the breakfast bar, where Calvin wore a grin. "Oh. It's on."

She grabbed a fistful of pumpkin guts and flung it at Calvin. The goo hit the side of his head, wetting his hair. Seeds coated his golden locks, and Rosie laughed until another mass of guts hit the front of her shirt. She whipped her head around to Ian, who giggled wildly.

"Gross. Ian, what are you doing?" Ethan flicked a stray seed from his shirt.

Rosie grabbed another handful of pumpkin guts and flung it at Ethan.

His jaw dropped, and his eyes widened as he looked down at his ruined shirt. "Hey!" His face reddened in anger, and he grabbed some goo and whipped it at Rosie's face. It hit her forehead with a splat, and Ethan's anger melted away as he laughed.

A pumpkin-gut fight ensued, and soon everyone was covered in slime.

"Okay, okay. Truce!" Rosie called. "Let's get these pumpkins carved!"

Rosie reached for the knife, ready to slice into her pumpkin, but it was gone.

"Yay!" Ian's voice beside her drew her attention, and she spotted the knife in his hand as he aimed it at his pumpkin, dangerously close to the other hand that he used to steady it.

"No, Ian!"

Rosie was too late. He stabbed the knife into the

pumpkin, slicing through the fleshy part of his hand between his thumb and forefinger.

A piercing scream was followed by a heart-wrenching wail. Rosie gasped as blood gushed from Ian's hand.

TWENTY-SEVEN
ROSIE

Rivulets of bright-red blood pulsed from Ian's hand and trailed down his arm at an alarming rate. Rosie froze, staring at the gaping wound.

"Ian!"

Ethan's panicked voice snapped Rosie from her trance, and she took action, reaching for Ian's hand. The warm, healing energy from within immediately worked its way through her arms and out her fingertips.

Ian's cries ceased as the pain disappeared from his face. Confusion replaced the agony, and he examined his hand before looking up at Rosie, his eyes stricken with fear. He pouted as fresh, silent tears poured from his eyes, and his chin wobbled. He quickly ran to Ethan's side, burying his face in his brother's shirt.

Ethan and Calvin stared at Rosie with rounded eyes and slack jaws. Their fear and astonishment polluted the air.

"What..." Calvin swallowed before he spoke again. "How did you do that?"

"She's a witch!" Ethan pointed at her. "Uncle Bruce told me. I didn't believe him, but it's true. She's a witch! A real witch!"

Rosie's hand flew to her mouth, and tears stung her eyes. She took a step back, fear knotting in her stomach. What had she done? They knew about her. What would the Cramers do to her? Would they go to the Council?

"Ethan, shut up!" Calvin scolded him. He turned to Ethan and grabbed him by the shirt. "You can't say anything. Not to Bruce, not to Dad. Don't say anything to anybody!"

"Why not?" Ian asked, casting a cautious glance in Rosie's direction.

Ethan narrowed his eyes.

"Ian." Calvin touched Ian's shoulder and bent down to his level. "Rosie has superpowers, but we have to keep them a secret so that she doesn't get in trouble, okay? She made you all better. You don't want her to get in trouble for that, do you?"

Ian shook his head as he stared at Rosie. A small smile spread across his face. "You have superpowers? Like Superman?"

Unable to speak, Rosie swallowed.

"Just like Superman, Ian," Calvin said. "But you remember how Superman had to keep his powers a secret? We have to keep Rosie's powers a secret too."

Calvin eyed Ethan, who was still glaring at Rosie. "Right, Ethan?" When Ethan didn't say anything, Calvin nudged him. "She helped Ian. You owe it to her to keep her secret, right?"

Ethan continued to stare at Rosie, ignoring Calvin. Finally, he nudged his brother. "Come on, Ian. Let's get you cleaned up."

The boys took off for the stairs then ran up the steps to their room. Rosie watched them go, her heart hammering. She darted her gaze back to Calvin.

He watched her for a few moments before he

stepped forward and pulled her into a warm hug. "Thank you."

For a moment, Rosie let her arms hang loosely at her sides as he held her, but then she melted into his embrace, wrapping her arms around him and squeezing tightly. His positive energy eased some of the panic thundering through her body. Her words were muffled as she nuzzled her face into his shoulder. "Your family is going to freak."

"I'll talk to the boys again and make sure they keep quiet." He pulled back and smiled at her. "I won't let them burn you at the stake."

As they finished cleaning up the mess in the kitchen, Rosie felt eyes on her. Glancing toward the stairs, she spotted Ian sitting on the bottom step, watching her. He eyed her with an expression of awe, like he was looking at a superhero.

Rosie smiled at him and waved her fingers. He waved back and gave a bright smile.

"Ian, come on!" Ethan pounded down the stairs and grabbed Ian's arm. He pinned her with an irritated stare, and the suspicious energy that emanated from him hit her like a slap to the face.

Abomination.

The word echoed in her head as he looked at her. She lowered her gaze and finished wiping pumpkin goo from the countertop.

"Hey."

She jerked her head toward Calvin.

"You want to get out of here?"

"God, yes."

"I have an idea."

Calvin motioned for her to follow as he headed toward the front door. "Do you want to drive?"

"I guess that depends on where we're going."

"I'll give you directions as we go. I thought maybe you might like to see the family business."

They headed outside and climbed into Rosie's Jeep. She fired up the engine and drove slowly down the winding path to the road. Calvin played with the radio, finding a local station to listen to. As they approached the road, he directed her to take a right turn. She accelerated, and Calvin rolled the window down. He leaned forward, letting the wind whip through his hair. Like a dog on a car ride, he smiled, and his eyes lit with excitement.

He gave her directions as they drove several miles down a series of roads that grew more and more desolate. The trees began to thin, and Rosie's mood started to sour.

"Where are we going?" she asked impatiently.

"We're almost there. Take a right up here."

Ahead, a dirt road was barely noticeable. As she turned onto it, her mood soured even more. Her stomach knotted, and her head started to pound. The dirt road wound up a small hill, and as the Jeep crested the top, Rosie's breath caught in her throat. She slammed on the brakes.

"You can park anywhere. This is the closest clearing site to the house. There are several south of here, but they're at least a forty-five-minute drive. Welcome to the family business."

As far as the eye could see, stumps sat like small gravestones in the dirt. Logging trucks loaded with the bare carcasses of what had once been magnificent trees lined the edges of the space. Rosie's stomach churned and coiled tightly.

Death. Death, everywhere.

Tears pricked her eyes as she looked out to a space devoid of life. Her mind went to the forest behind her house. All the life that depended on the trees. The birds, the squirrels, the deer...just a few of the hundreds of living things that were now without a home.

And the trees. Their untimely deaths echoed through the air like a toxic cloud.

A sob escaped, and her hand flew to her mouth as tears fell down her cheeks.

"Hey." Calvin placed a hand on her arm, and she jerked away from his touch. He snapped his hand back, and his face scrunched in confusion. "What is it? What's wrong?"

"I have to get out of here." Rosie's voice wavered as she threw the Jeep into reverse. Her hands shook as she gripped the steering wheel. Light-headed, she closed her eyes for a moment before she hit the gas pedal. "I can't be here. I can't see this."

"Rosie, I don't understand. What's wrong?"

Her head spun, and she hit the brakes. "I don't feel so good."

She threw the car into park and barely had time to open the door before she expelled her breakfast onto the ground. The sound of a car door slamming behind her barely registered in her mind before Calvin was suddenly in front of her, holding her hair back as she got sick again.

After a few moments, she leaned back into the Jeep, resting her head against the seat. Another sob wracked her body. "I need to go home. Now. Please?"

"Of course," Calvin said. "I'll drive."

Rosie nodded wearily as she climbed into the passenger seat. She lay her head against the cool glass of the window as Calvin steered the Jeep down the hill and back out to the main road. As they drove farther away, Rosie's head began to clear, and the queasiness in her stomach eased. She sat up a little straighter and glanced at Calvin. He caught her looking at him, and a muscle jumped in his jaw.

"Are you going to tell me what that was?"

"I don't know," Rosie said. "I got sick."

"Yeah, I gathered that. Are you okay now?"

"I think so."

"You didn't get sick until we got there," Calvin said quietly. "Was it something—"

"Please. I can't explain what that was. Can you just promise never to take me back there again?"

"Of course," Calvin said quietly. "I promise."

The rest of the drive was silent as Rosie stared out the window and tried to fight the fog of depression that lingered.

"I'VE NEVER FELT ANYTHING LIKE IT," ROSIE whispered.

Lucas brushed the hair back from her face. His touch soothed some of the ache that had settled deep inside her bones the moment she'd seen the dead forest. While the sickness had passed when she left the forest behind, the ache remained, both physical, causing a pain in her joints, and emotional, causing a depression she couldn't shake.

"I've never seen you like this," Lucas said. "You don't look good."

Rosie narrowed her eyes at him.

"I just mean you look ill." Lucas sighed. "So this was all because you saw some chopped-down trees? You've seen that before around here. Michael and Daniel trim and clear trees all the time."

"But not like this." Rosie shook her head in frustration.

He didn't understand. How could he? She didn't share much of the witch part of her life with anyone, even Lucas. They only knew what she let them see.

A headache pounded behind her eyes, and she

rubbed her forehead. "Maybe I'll feel better tomorrow."

"Maybe it wasn't the trees at all." Lucas's forehead creased. "Maybe you're getting the flu or something."

She wanted to cry. Lucas was such a huge part of her life. It killed her that this was something she couldn't share with him. There was only one person who could help her.

"I need to see my grandma. I'll go over to her house tomorrow after school."

Lucas nodded. "I can ride home with Sam."

"Or..."

"Or what?"

"Or...you could come with me."

Rosie bit her lip. He'd never met her grandma. She liked the idea of introducing him, even if it was while she felt like crap.

"If you want me there, I'll be there."

THE WORST MONDAY in the history of Mondays followed the next day. Lucas urged her to stay home that morning, commenting again that she didn't look well.

She didn't *feel* well.

Still, she plowed through her day with as much energy as she could muster. The fog in her brain made it nearly impossible to concentrate. A headache pounded against her temples.

During biology, Mason eyed her warily. "You're not going to hurl on me, are you?"

By the end of the day, she had an incredible urge to crawl under a blanket and sleep her life away.

Lucas took one look at her when she met him at the Jeep after school and ordered her to hand over the keys. He drove through town and out to the highway. When Rosie pointed out her grandmother's driveway, he turned the Jeep up the small gravel path that led to the cottage.

Clara emerged from the front door as Rosie slid out of the Jeep. Her grandmother smiled brightly at Lucas, but as she ran her eyes over Rosie, her brow creased.

"What happened?" Clara demanded, rushing to her side. "Rosie, your energy...it's so dismal."

As Clara ushered her into the house, Rosie explained the visit to the cleared forest and the sickness that had followed.

"Oh, darling," Clara gushed as she eased Rosie onto the couch. "Your empathy is even more powerful than I imagined."

As Clara ran her hands over her head, Rosie closed her eyes. Her grandmother's comfort and guidance warmed her. She missed this. She missed it so much. Opening her eyes, she looked up into her grandma's face. Clara's eyes misted as they bonded in their shared emotion. Her grandmother had missed it too. She'd told Rosie she had nothing more to offer her. No further guidance. It wasn't true. Rosie would always need her grandmother.

"What's wrong with her?" Lucas asked anxiously.

Clara smiled warmly at Lucas then turned back to Rosie and held her hand tightly. Her euphoric energy passed to Rosie, and she sighed in relief. The fog cleared from her mind, and the depression lifted like someone wiping a dark cloud away to reveal the sun.

As her body relaxed, she lay back against the couch cushions. Clara patted her hand.

"She'll be all right." Clara touched Lucas's knee. "Rosie feels things much more strongly than the rest of us. All witches do. But her empathy is exceptional. This would have passed in a few days, but it's good that she came. I can make it better right now." She smiled proudly as she patted Rosie's hand again.

When Lucas's eyes flitted to Rosie, something shifted in the blue depths of his stare. An awareness that wasn't there before. When his stare lingered for more than a minute, her cheeks heated.

"I'm feeling a lot better, Grandma," Rosie said. "Thank you."

"So, are you going to introduce me? I'm assuming this handsome young man is Lucas." She turned to him. "I've heard so much about you that I feel like I know you."

"Sorry, Grandma." Rosie sat up. "This is Lucas. Lucas, meet my grandma, Clara."

"I'm so glad I finally get to meet you," Clara gushed. "Can I get you something?"

Lucas shook his head. "No, thank you, ma'am."

Clara winked at Rosie. "He's handsome, *and* he has manners. I'll bet he's a good kisser too."

Rosie's eyes rounded, and she suddenly felt the urge to crawl under the floorboards. "Grandma!"

Sam yawned as his gaze wandered over the room. Council meetings were the worst. His father had been forcing him to attend over the last year, insisting that he get more familiar with the townspeople and the business that was brought before the council each month.

Easements, land permits, construction projects—it was all so *boring*. Even math class wasn't this bad.

"Next order of business, Paul Lewis has requested rezoning of the patch of state property south of his land. The land is currently marked as a no-hunting zone and... Paul, how many times do we have to tell you that the town council can't rezone state property?"

Sam scowled as Paul stood. Pompous ass had the nerve to show his face here?

"I wouldn't have to ask for the council's help to rezone the state land if eighty percent of the land around town didn't belong to Simon Hart! When is he going to give up some of his land so us hunters have a place to go?"

"Or at least let us hunt on his land!" someone from the crowd called out.

A chorus of agreement spread through the room, and Sam sank lower in his seat. This could get ugly. His father sat at the front of the room with the other council members. A muscle ticked in Simon's jaw, the only sign he was fazed by what was quickly becoming an angry mob. Bearded men in Carhartt overalls and blaze-orange stocking caps gestured wildly as they voiced their grievances in low tones.

"Simon Hart has the right to refuse hunters on his land." Ed, the council president, sat straighter in his chair as he tried to make his voice heard over the mumbled grumbles in the crowd. He cast a sidelong glance at Simon. "As much as we don't like it."

"We go through this every year," Simon said with a loud sigh. "My family has owned this land for generations. We have never allowed hunting, and we never will. So you'll have to drive a little farther to go hunting. Is that really so bad?"

"Your land has some of the best hunting for miles!" Paul yelled. "And I know for a fact there's a pack of wolves wandering these parts. What about the livestock around here? They're in danger if you let those wolves wander freely on your land."

"When was the last time we had an issue with livestock getting picked off by wolves?" Simon crossed his arms. "You're full of shit, Lewis."

"Tell them about the red wolf, Paul!" someone shouted.

For the first time, Simon lost his composure. His mocking smile turned into a worried frown then quickly morphed to anger. Sam's heart sped.

"There's a red wolf wandering around on your land, Hart!"

"All the more reason not to allow hunting on it, Lewis," Simon spat. "Red wolves are endangered."

"The population of wolves in Northern Wisconsin is growing," Paul challenged. "The DNR even raised the quota this year. They're looking for a big harvest to keep those pests under control."

A few shouts erupted as the hunters' disgruntled rumblings escalated. Simon shifted his gaze around the room. He laughed and shook his head before he fixed his eyes on the back wall.

"I understand you're all frustrated. Deer season is coming up, and you all want to take your boys out for a nice weekend of hunting." Simon sighed. "I have nothing against hunting. Our family hunts too. But I don't want hunters on my land. Tourists travel from all over the state and the country to hike the trails we have marked around Mingan Lake, and they don't want a bunch of crazy locals in blaze orange shooting at them."

"Screw the tourists!" Mr. Tompkins shouted. The short, balding man was the owner of the liquor store outside town. His place sat on prime real estate—right up the road from dozens of rental cabins.

"Screw the tourists?" Simon's eyes widened, and he chuckled. "Bob, do you really think your store would stay afloat without vacationers? Everyone in town knows beer is cheaper at the grocery store. Your business depends on the naive tourists who pay an arm and a leg for the convenience of a store steps away from the cabins so that they don't have to drive their drunk asses into town. No one from around here is dumb enough to shop at your store."

Bob rolled his eyes as everyone laughed. Someone gave him a playful shove, and Bob swatted his beefy hand at them.

"Tourism brings a lot of revenue into this town," Simon continued.

The laughter died down. Sam looked around at a sea of amused smiles on faces that had been surly with anger moments before. His father had a way with people. "Where do you think they go to eat and shop when they come here? They bring their money to town. I didn't hear anyone complaining last year when tourism dollars paid for the new pool at the high school."

Silence filled the room, and a few people nodded.

"I know it means you have to travel a little farther to go hunting, but my stance hasn't changed. No hunting will be allowed on Hart property. Not now. Not ever."

Reluctant agreement replaced the previous hostility. No one could argue Simon's point. An impressed smile lit Sam's face until his gaze landed on Paul Lewis. The man's face was red with rage.

"Ugh." Becca moaned. "These are all ugly."

"I think we're going to have to go the traditional-black-hat-and-dress route." Rosie pulled out a witch costume that had been wedged between a clown getup and a werewolf one-piece. Halloween decor flooded the walls and corners of the costume shop—gravestones, cobwebs, ghosts, and goblins with glowing red eyes—and spooky ghost whistles blared from the overhead speakers.

"That's so boring, though!" Becca whined. "And *I'm* not painting my face green."

"But it was okay to make me paint my face green?" Rosie raised an eyebrow. "I see how it is."

"Maybe we can drive to Rhinelander this weekend." Becca eyed the witch costume with a wrinkled nose. "I'm sure we can find something better there."

"I can't." Rosie frowned.

"Come on. Can't you skip the family thing for one weekend?"

Tilting her head, Rosie raised her eyebrows and put her hand on her hip.

"Okay, okay." Becca relented, holding her hands

up. "I get it. You can't. I'll go myself. I'll find something great. We'll look like sexy bitches."

A snort of laughter startled Rosie, and she spun around to face a group of girls standing a few feet behind her. She recognized Cassie among the group, and anger coiled inside her.

Cassie ran her eyes up and down Rosie's body. "Don't waste your time, Becca. Rosie doesn't need a costume to show up as the town freak."

A round of laughter brought a triumphant smile to Cassie's face. Her strong emotions made the hair on the back of Rosie's neck rise. Disdain, jealousy, and a charged-up energy—Cassie was looking for a fight. It poured from her.

As much as Rosie would have loved to wipe the floor with her, she'd just finished a fight with Lucas about this. And her father was adamant about keeping a low profile, which included staying out of fights. Then there was her grandmother's voice in her head beckoning her to turn the other cheek.

Rosie's stomach tightened as she turned her back to the girls, carefully placing the costume back on the rack. She was used to the teasing. Most of the time, it didn't faze her. Who cared what these small-town, closed-minded imbeciles thought? But when the teasing happened in front of people she cared about, the embarrassment was real. And it hurt.

And when it came from Cassie, it was really, really hard to ignore. Every time Cassie flirted with Lucas, Rosie wanted to scratch her eyes out. Just thinking about it made her hands ball into fists.

Something within her snapped She spun around and took two long strides forward, planting herself in front of the tall, dark-haired girl. "Town freak is better than town slut. No amount of makeup can hide that hideous mug, Cassie."

Cassie's jaw dropped before she clamped her mouth shut. Rosie winced at the familiarity of the emotions that rolled off Cassie—embarrassment, hurt, rejection. She'd dealt with those same feelings for years. Knowing she'd caused them for someone else made her feel sick.

Anger swept over Cassie, and she crossed her arms. "Ha! I think you have us all beat in the town slut department. How about it, Rosie? Still stalking Mason like the little freak you are?"

"Back off, Cassie," Becca growled. "You know as well as everyone that he's full of it. Unless what he said about the two of you in the back seat of his Mustang is true?"

A tense silence followed. Cassie put her hand on her hip and scowled. Embarrassment rolled off her in waves.

"That's what I thought," Becca snapped. She grabbed Rosie's arm. "Come on. Let's go."

As they stepped out of the dark shop and into the bright sunlight, Rosie squinted. She could barely keep up with Becca as she dragged her down the sidewalk, away from the Halloween store. She almost tripped over a planter full of bright-orange marigolds.

"Holy shit, Rosie!" Becca turned to her. "Nice comeback!"

Rosie exhaled, and her shoulders slumped. "I shouldn't have done that."

"Um, yes! It was awesome!" Becca nudged her. "You know you're allowed to stick up for yourself, but you never do. I don't know why you put up with so much crap."

Rosie shrugged. Her gaze wandered to the displays of pumpkins and flowers that decorated the sidewalks and storefronts. "Usually, it doesn't bother me so much. Why should I care what other people think about me?"

"You shouldn't." Becca sighed and looked to the sky. "I guess I just wish everyone else knew you like I do. That's all."

"They do know me." Rosie grinned. "You're just the only one crazy enough to like me the way I am."

Becca laughed and threw her arm around Rosie's shoulder. "Maybe that's because you're the only one crazy enough to like me the way *I* am. Let's get some ice cream."

THIRTY-ONE
ROSIE

Cold dread coursed through Rosie's body as she neared Cramer House the following Saturday. She hadn't spoken more than three words to Calvin since they left the cleared forest the previous weekend. Just knowing that awful place was a few measly miles away made her stomach roil.

Just like every other weekend, he waited for her at the gate. She took a deep breath as she parked the Jeep and waited for him to climb into the passenger seat.

As he fastened his seat belt, he gave her a cautious smile. "There's somewhere I want to take you."

Rosie set her jaw. "The last time you took me somewhere, it didn't go so well. As much as it pains me to say it, I'd rather stay here."

"You'll like this. I know you will."

Rosie studied him for a few moments before she nodded slowly. She backed the car out to the road and followed Calvin's instructions, taking them south.

"It was the trees, wasn't it?" Calvin asked quietly. "A lot of people don't like the idea of cutting down trees, but it was different for you. It made you sick. Why?"

"I can't really explain it, Calvin." Rosie kept her eyes on the road. "Just promise me we're not going back there."

"I promise." Calvin grinned. "Something tells me you'll really like where we're going."

"If you say so." Rosie forced a small smile. "Isn't your dad going to be angry we're missing lunch?"

Calvin shrugged. "I told him where I was taking you."

"And he was okay with it?"

"He's proud of the family business. I think he likes the idea of me showing it off to you."

Her muscles tensing, Rosie gripped the steering wheel. Anger coursed through her. "The family business? As in the family business of cutting down trees? You said you weren't taking me there, Calvin."

"Relax." Calvin held his hands up, his eyes pleading. "Cutting down trees isn't all we do. We're werewolves, Rosie, the same as you and your family. We depend on the cover of the forest. We always give back what we take."

"What do you mean?"

"Pull in here." Calvin pointed out a driveway ahead.

Fear coiled in her stomach. All her instincts told her to turn the car around and drive back to Cramer House, drop Calvin off, and go home. Fighting her fear, she turned onto a dirt road much like the dirt road she'd turned onto last weekend.

As she crested the hill, her heart sped. The skyline was vacant, confirming her fear that the forest had been cleared. She was about to rip Calvin a new one, but something made her pause. She drove forward, and the energy she felt wasn't death. It was life. New life.

As far as she could see, saplings sprang from the dirt, soaking up the sun.

"When we clear trees, we always replant," Calvin said. "It keeps the forests healthy."

A smile tugged at her lips as she glanced at Calvin. She opened her door and jumped out of the Jeep, approaching the edge of the new growth of trees.

Most of the saplings were taller than she was, but a few were small—most likely grown naturally after the others had been planted. Rosie knelt next to one that looked thin and frail. Not strong enough to survive the upcoming winter.

Closing her eyes, she reached out to the sapling and focused on its weak energy. She let her own energy feed it, and she smiled as she felt the sapling become strong. When she opened her eyes, her smile widened. The weak little tree towered over the others.

She turned to Calvin and laughed at his astonished expression.

"That kind of growth takes years. How did you..." He shook his head. "You find new ways to surprise me every time I see you."

Rosie basked in the light, happy energy surrounding her. The trees were young and strong, and the new growth brought other new life. Ferns, grass, moss, and lichen formed the underbrush while wildflower roots went dormant for the winter, waiting to bloom fresh in the spring. Mice scurried under the grass, and rabbits nibbled on thick plants. In the distance, a fox sniffed at the ground, searching for lunch.

She closed her eyes and took a deep breath. Suddenly, a dark shadow of anger dampened the positive energy. Her eyes popped open as she heard the hard, familiar voice.

"I knew it." Bruce stomped over the grass toward them. His stormy expression sent a chill up her spine. "Witch. You're a freak witch."

Rosie jumped to her feet and stumbled backward.

"Bruce, what are you doing here?" Calvin positioned himself in front of Rosie.

"I heard you tell your dad where you were taking her." Bruce's lip curled, and his nostrils flared. "I knew I had to keep an eye on you. Make sure the two of you didn't do anything stupid. Imagine my surprise to see this."

Bruce took a step forward and pointed at Rosie. "The rumor is true. He told me, and I had my doubts, but it's true. You were born from a witch. A real witch."

Her mind racing, Rosie wondered who *he* was. Who told Bruce her mother was a witch? No one outside the pack knew about her.

"William thinks it's a good idea to start a whole generation of offspring from you? Freak witch-wolf pups?" Bruce shook his head. "You have to be stopped. You have to be stopped right now."

Bruce barreled toward her, and panic took over, freezing Rosie in place. She reached out to the energy around her, focusing, calling for help.

As Bruce neared her, his feet tangled in the underbrush around him. Vines rapidly wound around his legs, working their way up past his knees. He stumbled, staring down in shock. He stared back up at Rosie, his face red with anger. "What are you doing, witch? Stop! Stop!"

Rosie focused on the twisting branches. She concentrated on wrapping them around and around his legs. Vines worked their way up, around his waist, squeezing. He screamed as the vines rose toward his throat then twisted around his reddened neck. Blue veins bulged as he choked on their strong hold.

"Rosie, stop!"

Hands grabbed her arm, but she shook them off. A muffled curse followed, then the hands were back on her arms again, and she found herself staring into Calvin's eyes. His green irises were pleading. "Please, Rosie, don't do this! Don't kill him. It's not you. You're not a killer."

Rosie sucked in a deep breath. He was right. What was she doing?

Bruce fell to his knees, struggling to breathe, and she let go of her hold on the plants. They fell away from him just as quickly as they had twisted their way up his body.

Bruce tumbled forward on all fours, heaving in mouthfuls of air. He raised his head slowly toward Rosie, his face red with fury. His eyes glowed yellow. In a flash of movement, he morphed into a large brown wolf.

Rosie's heart dropped, and she turned to run, shifting to wolf form midstride. Her legs pumped as fast as she could make them go, but she was no match for his pace or his strength. She felt his hot breath on her back seconds before his immense weight took her down, and she felt sharp teeth sink into her flesh.

THIRTY-TWO

ROSIE

Rosie had felt the bite of a wolf several times but never in anger. Warning bites, playful bites. Those were nothing like the pain she felt when Bruce's teeth pierced her flesh. She cried out as he ripped fur and skin from her front leg and took her down to the ground. They rolled across the grass before he was back on top of her in a flash, biting at her legs, her chest. She bared her teeth and snapped back at him, but he had her pinned.

He reared back and bared his bloodstained teeth, and Rosie's stomach dropped. She was going to die. He was going to kill her. She would never see Lucas again. For some reason, that part scared her more than death. She cried out, and as he lunged toward her throat, she closed her eyes and waited.

But death didn't come.

Before his teeth could sink in, the weight of Bruce's body left her chest. Her breath caught as her eyes popped open, and she watched a second wolf tackle Bruce to the ground.

Calvin.

They twisted into each other, biting and tearing

flesh. Yelps pierced the air, but Rosie wasn't sure which of them was crying out. She stumbled to her feet and backed away, putting distance between herself and the fight.

She wanted to help, but she feared she would only be in the way. Watching helplessly as they continued to tear into each other, she silently urged Calvin on, praying he would gain the advantage.

Her heart thundered, and she yelped in sympathy as Bruce pinned Calvin, but in a move so swift that she almost didn't see it, Calvin spun Bruce onto his back and sank his teeth into his uncle's neck.

Bruce yowled in pain, but Calvin's hold tightened as he shook his head.

Rosie's stomach tanked, and she worried that Calvin might do what he'd just convinced her not to. She took a step forward, and his anger hit her hard. Years of pent-up frustration emanated from him as he clenched his teeth around Bruce's neck. Bruce cried out again, and Rosie knew she had to do something.

She shifted to human form, shivering as the cold air touched her bare skin. With a shaking hand, she reached forward and touched Calvin's furry back, letting her calming energy wash over him. His tense muscles relaxed, and he unclenched his jaw, loosening his hold on Bruce.

Bruce flopped back into the dirt, panting heavily. Blood coursed out of his neck, but he was alive. As Calvin's energy softened, Rosie pulled her hand away and quickly morphed back into wolf form.

He turned toward her and paused. His head swiveled back to Bruce. She could feel the emotion coming off him. The rage was gone, replaced by shock and fear. He took a step forward and nuzzled her. *"Thank you, Rosie."*

Rosie pressed her head into his neck. He wouldn't become another Cramer monster, not if she could help it.

Fortunately, Rosie had a nice big blanket in the back seat of her Jeep to cover herself with on the ride back to Cramer House. During the drive, Calvin called his father to let him know what had happened. As horrible as Bruce was, they had to get him help for his injuries. They'd left him bleeding out on the ground.

When they returned to Cramer House, William and George had already left to retrieve Bruce. Calvin pulled the Jeep to the front of the house and cut the engine. He exhaled a shaky breath as he stared out the windshield. His face, chest, and arms were a mess of cuts and scratches. Rosie placed a hand on his shoulder. His brow pinched in confusion.

She let her healing energy flow into him, and the injuries disappeared from his skin.

His green eyes lit in amazement, and he smiled. "I don't suppose you can heal yourself? Your arm looks like it really hurts."

Deep puncture marks marred the top of Rosie's arm where Bruce had bitten her. Pain throbbed up her arm and through her shoulder. "I can't heal myself."

"Why don't we go get dressed, and I'll bandage your arm."

Rosie nodded, and they moved slowly into the house and up the stairs. When Rosie closed the door to her bedroom, she took a deep breath and tried to fight the urge to curl up in her bed and cry. Her hands shook as she fished a pair of jeans and a T-shirt out of her duffel and got dressed. A tank top would have been easier for dressing her wound, but she didn't have one with her.

When she made her way downstairs, Calvin was already sitting at the breakfast bar with a first aid kit. He patted the stool next to him. "I promise to be gentle."

Gauze, alcohol, scissors, and tape were laid out on the counter. Rosie reluctantly sat down next to him and rolled up her sleeve. He hissed in sympathy when he got a good look at the wound.

"I called your dad," Calvin said as he reached for the alcohol.

Rosie's eyes widened. "What? Why would you do that?"

Her dad couldn't know about this. If he found out, he would come, and if he came, there could be fighting. He would forbid her from coming back, which would get him in trouble with the Council. What would they do to him?

Calvin's eyebrows shot to his hairline. "Why? What do you mean, '*why*'? Why *wouldn't* I call your dad? I mean, my dad wouldn't care if something bad happened to me, but your dad strikes me as the type to give a crap."

Rosie huffed. The damage was done. No doubt, Simon was on his way. Probably halfway to Cramer

House by now. Worry formed tight knots in her stomach. "Never mind."

Calvin knit his brow then shrugged before going to work on her arm.

~

Two HOURS LATER, Rosie and Calvin lounged on the couch in the sitting room. She wanted nothing more than to go home, but if her father was on his way, she needed to stay and make sure everything went okay.

The front door flew open, and William burst through. Behind him, George half carried, half dragged a bandaged and bleeding Bruce into the house.

"Take him upstairs." William's voice was low. His eyes found Rosie's, and they blazed with anger. "Bruce told us what happened."

Beside her, Calvin's terrified energy touched her with devastating force. His voice wavered as he said, "He tried to kill Rosie."

"Because she's a witch!" William hissed angrily. "She lied to us. Deceived us."

The hammering of Rosie's heart was loud in her ears. Tears pricked her eyes.

"Witches are cunning, conniving harlots. They abandoned werewolves years ago, and good riddance. They're the worst females alive. It's too bad the witch hunts didn't wipe them all out. She's just like the rest of them. She can't be trusted."

"No!" Calvin stood from the couch. "Don't talk about her like that."

"Sit down and shut up!" William barely looked at Calvin. "Stupid piece of—"

Anger boiled in her veins, and Rosie shot to her feet. "Stop! You are the worst person alive! How can you treat him like that?"

William's eyes rounded, and a smile crept across his face. "Because even you have more balls than he does."

"Leave her alone." Calvin's voice sounded steadier. "Just let her go home."

"Go home?" William laughed. "Oh no, no, no. She's not going home. I've got a place for her in the basement cells with the other girls. She can wait there until the Council gets here to deal with her."

"Touch her, and it will be the last thing you ever do!" Simon shouted from the doorway, startling everyone.

Behind him, Sam scanned the room until his eyes landed on Rosie. Relief washed over his face, and he gave her a small smile.

Simon stepped forward, into the foyer, his furious glare trained on William. "You dare to threaten my daughter?"

Rosie's breath hitched. Fear for her father competed with the relief of seeing him.

"Simon. I didn't realize you were coming." William straightened. "I believe we have some issues to discuss. Your daughter—"

"Is coming home with me." Simon's voice dripped with contempt. "Unless you would like me to tell the Council that Bruce tried to kill her, and you threatened to imprison her." He stepped forward. "I may have kept a few details about her from them, but trust me, she's still a prize in their eyes... and in the World Council's eyes. Imagine their anger if they found out the Cramers tried to kill the only living female werewolf ever to have walked the earth. I don't think that would go well for you, William."

Warmth filled the cold, hollow, lonely pit she'd felt inside for so long. This was the father she remembered. Her pillar of strength. He was still there. Still strong as ever. How could she have doubted him?

William cleared his throat and adjusted his collar. "It seems we both have a little something we'd like to keep under wraps. Perhaps—"

"Rosie, let's go." Simon didn't take his eyes off William.

Rosie looked at Calvin. Fear for him cramped her stomach.

Tears clouded his eyes, but he smiled and nodded. "I'll be okay, Rosie. Go."

A lump formed in her throat, and she stepped toward him. "You're a strong, brave, amazing person, Calvin. Don't let him tell you that you aren't."

Tears dripped down Calvin's face, and when Rosie kissed his cheek, their salty wetness lingered on her lips. She reached for his hand and squeezed it before she turned to go.

William's gaze trailed over to Rosie as she crossed the foyer to the door, and the sneer of distaste he aimed her way brought the sting of tears to her eyes. Damn him. How did he have that power over her? Why couldn't she heed her own advice? She shouldn't care what he thought of her.

Sadly, she did. She could tell herself over and over that she didn't care what anyone thought...but she did. She really did. And the pain of their judgement was paralyzing.

~

SAM DROVE Rosie's Jeep back to Hart House, and Rosie rode in her father's car. She kept her gaze fixed out the window as they drove in silence. The yellows, reds, and oranges of fall foliage popped against the orange glow of the early-evening sky. It was breathtaking. How could so much beauty exist in such an ugly world?

"How's your arm?" Her father's voice was quiet, but she could feel his concern.

She studied him for a moment as he kept his stare on the road. "It hurts a little, but it's not bad."

He nodded, and a muscle in his jaw moved as he clenched his teeth. Something she noticed he did whenever something seemed to bother him.

"How long has Bruce been bothering you?"

"He hasn't really been bothering me. He just doesn't hide that he hates me."

Simon kept his stare forward as he spoke. "Has he ever harmed you before?"

She chewed on the inside of her cheek. Telling Simon about the day they'd played hide and seek would only make things worse, but lying wasn't an option. Her father—her alpha—demanded the truth.

"He shoved me once. Calvin stopped him before it went any further."

The muscle in his jaw jumped again, and silence followed for a few moments before he finally spoke again. "Did Calvin ever do anything to you?"

"No." Rosie answered quickly. "We're friends. He's been good to me."

"Just friends?" Simon raised an eyebrow, but he still didn't look her way.

"Just friends."

Silence followed. When it was clear he wasn't going to say anything more, Rosie turned her gaze back to the window. Tears pooled in her eyes, and she wiped them away in frustration. She almost didn't ask, but the whispered words slipped from her. "Why do they hate me?"

"What?" Through the reflection in the passenger-side window, she could see him look her way.

"Why do they hate me? Bruce, William, Amos. Is it because I'm a girl? Because I'm a girl and a were-wolf? Because of my magic? All of the above? Why? What did I ever do to them?"

"They're afraid, Rosie," Simon said. "Afraid of what they don't know."

"That's stupid."

A soft chuckle. "I know it is. They're stupid."

Lucas paced the rec room. It took twelve steps to get from one end to the other. Inside, his mate bond roared. The normally pleasant warmth of the fire burned him from the inside out. Every nerve, every cell screamed with the need to have his mate home, safe, in his arms.

Rosie.

God, he prayed she was okay. He had been in the middle of watching a movie with Sam, Michael, and Daniel when Simon charged into the room, ordering Sam to go with him. As Sam stood from the couch, Simon explained that he'd received a call from Calvin Cramer. Something had happened to Rosie.

Lucas's heart stopped. Coldness spread through his limbs. What happened? For the past several hours, horrible scenarios had plagued his mind and buzzed in his ears like a swarm of bees.

"You're going to wear a hole in the carpet, Lucas." Daniel watched him pace. "Sit down."

"Yeah, man." Michael opened a can of beer. "Calm down. I'm sure she's fine."

Lucas paused to look at them. Daniel bounced his foot nervously on the coffee table, and Michael was on his fourth beer. At the game table, Stuart sat quietly. They were all worried too.

Roger strolled into the room, his hands in his pockets. He watched Lucas closely. "Has there been any word?"

The pity in his father's eyes frustrated him. He didn't need that. He needed Rosie here. Safe.

"Nothing," Daniel said.

"Dinner is ready," Martha said as she poked her head into the rec room. "I want everyone at the table in five minutes." She scowled at Lucas. "Everyone."

The pack members made their way out of the rec room to get cleaned up for dinner, but Lucas continued his pacing.

His father paused in the doorway. "Come on, son."

"I'm not hungry."

"I don't care. You're eating. End of story."

With a frustrated sigh, Lucas nodded and moved toward the hallway. As he turned the corner, the sound of the front door opening caused him to spin on his heel. Sam entered, his face impassive. Behind him, Simon escorted Rosie into the house. Her head hung low, her eyes on the floor.

Lucas held his breath as he ran his gaze over her. Scratches and bruises marred her cheeks and arms, and a large, blood-tinged bandage was wrapped around her upper arm. She looked tired. Really tired.

He wanted to ask what had happened, but he couldn't form the words. The muscles in his feet twitched, aching to run to her.

"What happened?" Roger asked, stepping forward to close the front door behind them.

"It's a long story," Simon said. "I smell dinner. Let's eat, and we can talk later."

"*Rosie?*" He couldn't make his voice work.

Rosie's head jerked up toward him. "*Lucas.*" Tears pooled in her eyes. "*The tree. After supper.*"

LUCAS WAS PACING AGAIN. Seemed to be all he could do today. Every once in a while, he would pause and touch the tree, as though maybe it had some answers for him.

Rosie's tree.

Dinner had been a firing squad of questions for Rosie. Simon spoke for her, answering everyone and filling them in. It took all of Lucas's willpower not to rush to her side as he heard the details.

She'd been in danger. Real danger. And he hadn't been there. It enraged him. She was his. How dare any other wolf lay a hand on her?

And what about the Council? Would William keep quiet?

One thing was for certain—the moment he turned eighteen, he would challenge Marcus Beckett.

The sound of light footsteps in the distance drew his attention, and he watched as Rosie stepped out of the yard. She paused as she looked at Lucas, and her face scrunched up in agony.

It was all he needed. He stepped forward, scooping her into his arms. He held her tightly, running his hand through her curls.

"Shh. It's okay. You're safe now."

"I was so scared."

"I know. I'm here."

"I thought I would never see you again," she whimpered. Sobs wracked her small frame as he tightened his hold.

"Hey," Lucas whispered as he pulled away. He took her face into his hands and wiped away her tears with his thumbs. "It's over now. You're okay. You're here. You're safe. It's over."

Rosie bobbed her head and sniffed then ran her fingers over Lucas's cheek. He closed his eyes and relished the feel of her presence. Leaning down, he brushed his lips over hers, and she answered him, kissing him deeply.

They melted to the ground, and Lucas breathed her in, aching with need. He broke the kiss and studied her face before he hugged her close to him. She laid her head against his chest, fingering the seam of his shirt.

Lucas leaned back against the oak and listened as she shared all the details of the day. The vibration of her voice against his chest was soothing. He stayed silent, letting her talk. When she was done, her exhaustion got the best of her, and she fell asleep in his arms.

He said a small prayer of thanks that she was home. He wanted nothing more than to keep her safe and swore to whoever was listening that he would.

THIRTY-FIVE
ROSIE

Becca's bedroom was vastly different from Rosie's. It had no plants, no candles, no incense burners. A vanity in the corner was covered in creams and varied makeup products. Clothes spilled out of her large closet and covered most of the floor and half her bed. Rosie knew from previous sleepovers that Becca never cleaned up the mess. Ever. The walls were painted pink and covered with collages of Becca and her friends. At least half of them were of Becca and Rosie.

Rosie had come by to try on the costume Becca picked up on her trip to Rhinelander last weekend. As much as Rosie despised shopping, it would have been a much better weekend than the one she experienced.

When she had turned up at school scratched and bruised, Becca asked her what happened. She'd thought up a lie quickly, telling her she'd fallen off an ATV.

Her friend had stared at her for almost a full minute before blinking in surprise. "Are you kidding me? Thank goodness you're okay!"

Everyone knew what had happened to her by

Monday afternoon, the result of a combination of small-town life and having a best friend who was the biggest gossip in the school.

"So, I couldn't find anything that looked like it came from *Wicked*, but I did find these, and I thought they were just too cute to pass up."

Rosie examined the costumes. Much prettier than anything they could have found in Hanks Hollow, that was for sure. One was purple with a sheer black overlay and silver stars and moons embellished on the front. A matching pointed hat had the same colors and patterns. The other had a black bodice over a red satin under piece. A full black skirt had red satin sewn into the folds.

"I call dibs on the purple one," Becca said. "Mostly because I don't think I'll fit into the black-and-red one." She gave a small smile. "I got that one in the juniors section."

Rosie's cheeks flushed. "It's okay. I like it."

"Come over Friday after school. I'll do your hair." Becca clapped and jumped up and down. "This is going to be so great!"

THE BUZZ of conversation at school centered around Friday's party. Not only did Halloween fall on a Friday this year, but it also fell on the night of a full moon.

Of course, that meant that Rosie had to find an excuse to duck out of the party early. She would be itching to change as soon as the moon lit the night. She could hold off for a couple of hours. The pack didn't typically go for a full-moon run until late at night. Still, the discomfort increased as the night wore on.

During first-period social studies, Rosie doodled small pictures in her notebook while the teacher droned on about something. She glanced at Lucas. He was slouched in his chair, exuding the *don't care* attitude, but she could tell he was listening to the lecture. Probably already knew all the material.

"Are you sure you don't want to go to the party Friday night?" She bit her lip. *"It would be so much more fun if you were there."*

He shuffled his feet and flitted his gaze to her. A small smile formed on his lips. *"Why? So we can feel the discomfort of not being able to touch each other* and *the discomfort of needing to shift? No, thank you."*

"Killjoy."

"That's me."

Rosie let out a huff and scowled at him. It was useless to try to talk him into it. Parties weren't his thing. Costumes weren't his thing. He would hate every minute of it.

During fourth period, Rosie tried her best to ignore Mason's whispered conversation with Jared, but it was like he was purposely whispering loudly enough to bother her.

"My dad and I got matching guns. We got our initials engraved on them too. Can't wait to use them. Gonna get me some venison, then I'm going to get me a nice red wolf pelt."

"Good luck with the wolf pelt," Jared whispered, casting a glance in Rosie's direction. "Simon Hart isn't going to let anyone hunt on his land. No one's getting that pelt this year."

"Yeah, we'll see about that."

Rosie snapped her head toward him and narrowed her eyes. Mason stared back at her with a mocking grin.

"You stay off my family's land," Rosie whispered.

"You going to make me? There's a lot of forest your dad owns. You going to watch every inch of it to make sure we don't hunt there?"

"Hey!" Mr. McCall shouted. "I've had enough of the talking during class. Quiet down now."

Rosie gritted her teeth as she glared at Mason. He winked at her.

Rosie's costume fit perfectly. The skirt hit her at the ankles, and the red silk top felt smooth against her skin. Becca helped her lace up the black bodice—a little tighter than she liked—and the finished product looked like it was made just for her.

Becca steered her to her vanity and pushed her into the seat. As she got to work on her hair, Rosie was reminded of Martha doing her hair last spring. The steady stream of gossip sounded familiar. When the topic of conversation turned to Cassie and Mason— two of Rosie's least favorite people in the world—her insides coiled with anxiety.

"I can't believe the nerve of Cassie and her stupid little entourage. Coming at you like that in the costume shop. Everyone knows she's done it with half the school, but I still know for a *fact* that Mason is lying about the two of them in the back of his Mustang. She wouldn't deny it if it were true. She's never tried to protect her rep before. I don't know why she would start now."

"Ugh." Rosie wrinkled her nose. "Can we talk about something else?"

"Yeah, yeah, sorry." Becca continued curling

Rosie's hair. "I was going to pin it up, but I think it will look nice down. What do you think?"

Lucas liked her hair down. He liked to play with it. Rosie smiled. "Yeah. Keep it down."

"You got it! All done."

Rosie stood next to Becca in front of the full-length mirror by the closet and smiled at their reflection. "You look beautiful, Becca."

"We both do!" She gave a dimpled smile, her blue eyes shining, as she hugged Rosie. "I love you, lady."

~

THE PARTY WAS in full swing when Rosie and Becca arrived. Crowds of people wandered through the park, dressed in costumes ranging from scary clowns to sexy nurses. Kids ran from booth to booth, playing carnival games and bobbing for apples.

A band played on the gazebo stage, and a dance floor stretched out in front of them. The firepit was alight with roaring flames, and people sat on hay bales, drinking cider and enjoying the music. Past the firepit, raucous laughter could be heard from the beer tent.

Rosie had a blast with Becca. They drank cider, ate caramel apples, and squeezed together into the photo booth for pictures.

As the evening wore on, Rosie started to feel the itch to change. She was ready to tell Becca it was time for her to go home, just as soon as she could find her. The social butterfly had been whisked away by one of her friends to get some cider. She'd promised to come right back, but that had been ten minutes ago. Rosie sat at one of the picnic tables and watched the dance floor, where people in costumes gyrated to the music.

"You look beautiful."

Rosie spun, searching the crowd for Lucas. Her heart danced happily, and she couldn't help the smile that spread across her face. *"Where are you?"*

A tap on her shoulder startled her, and she turned to find Lucas standing before her. No costume. He wore his typical T-shirt, jeans, and flannel. He looked amazing.

She stood and stared into his eyes. She was dying to kiss him.

"Dance with me?" He seemed uncertain.

Rosie looked around. "Are you sure? All these people—"

"I don't care," he blurted. "I need to hold you. I don't want to wait."

He took her hand and pulled her out to the dance floor. They pressed together, and she rested her head against his chest, listening to his heartbeat. Strong, steady.

As they swayed to the music, everything fell away. The people, the noises. It was just the two of them and the tune they were dancing to. Rosie closed her eyes and breathed in his scent as she listened to the music and felt his strong body against hers.

Perfect.

"Oh my God! I knew it!"

Becca's voice cut through the moment like a knife, and Rosie frowned as Lucas pulled away. She turned to her friend, her cheeks heating at the stares that came their way. Murmurs rippled over the crowd. The gossip had started. By the end of the night, the entire town would know.

"Becca, it's not—"

"Uh-huh." Becca crossed her arms and smiled. "I

totally called this a long time ago. Why didn't you tell me?"

"I have to go," Lucas said.

As he hurried through the crowd, Rosie watched him longingly. The dance had been perfect. By morning, her dad would know about them. News traveled fast. But it was worth it. She would face his wrath. Maybe they could tell him it was just an innocent dance.

"I'll see you at home." His voice in her head eased her anxiety as the people around her went back to dancing and talking.

Becca grabbed Rosie's hand and dragged her off the dance floor to the hay bales next to the firepit. "Tell me everything," Becca gushed. "Including why you kept it from me!"

Rosie took a deep breath. "We... I mean, it's not..."

"Stop," Becca said. Her brow furrowed angrily. "Don't try to tell me you're just friends. What I just saw on that dance floor wasn't two friends. It was two people in love."

Rosie sighed. "We've been trying to keep this a secret. I don't know how my dad would react."

It was the truth. Part of the truth, anyway.

"And I just called it to the attention of half the town." Becca smacked her forehead. "I'm so sorry, Rosie."

"You didn't know. I wish I could have told you a long time ago."

"Why didn't you? I wouldn't have told your dad." Becca looked hurt. "Come on."

"I know." Rosie frowned. God, how she wished she could have told her. "I'm sorry."

"Well, if it makes you feel any better, I don't think

that many people noticed. Or if they did, they didn't know what was going on."

Rosie nodded. "I better get home."

"Already?"

Rosie had started feeling the itch to change again. "Yeah. I'm tired. Thank you for everything, Becca. I really had a good time tonight."

"Hey." Becca grabbed Rosie's hand. "You're my best friend, Rosie. You can always tell me anything, okay?"

Guilt flooded her veins. All the secrets and lies over the years. She didn't deserve to have Becca as a friend. "I love you, Becca."

Becca hugged Rosie. "I want to hear everything. Tomorrow, okay? Come to my dad's restaurant for lunch. I want every juicy detail."

"I'll be there," Rosie said. "Promise."

THIRTY-SEVEN
ROSIE

THE MAGNETIC ENERGY OF THE BRIGHT, FULL moon pulled at Rosie. The stone surface of the patio reflected its light. Flowers in the garden glowed. Excitement hung in the air, shared by all the creatures, from the mice that scurried in the grass to the bats that bobbed and weaved through the trees. Starting at the very tips of her toes, a restless current ran through her body, up to her scalp, making her tingle. She needed to run.

"Wow. A moon goddess. It's my lucky night."

Rosie turned to find Lucas staring at her, his blue eyes twinkling and a playful smile on his lips.

"Ugh." She stuck her finger in her mouth to mimic vomiting. "That was so cheesy, Lucas."

He laughed and glanced over his shoulder before planting a kiss on her lips. It caught her off guard, and she didn't even have the chance to close her eyes before he pulled away again.

"Where is everyone?" Michael complained as he came out to the patio. "I'm getting itchy."

Daniel followed him out, and Stuart came next.

They started to take their clothes off, preparing for the change.

Rosie sat still in the chair. She would wait until the last minute to disrobe. Her relationship with Lucas left her feeling self-conscious.

"Everyone here?" Simon asked as he and Amos walked onto the patio, followed closely by Sam and Roger.

As always, Amos's energy fouled the air. He looked at her, and a strange smile played at his lips when he met her gaze.

Odd.

Simon looked around, counting heads, then grinned. "Let's go."

Rosie watched everyone leap off the patio, changing into wolf form. She threw off her clothes and followed suit, shifting midstride as she raced across the yard. Her father paused at the edge of the woods, watching everyone run by. He raised his head to the sky and let out a long, low *awooo*. They all paused, and the chorus of their howls rang through the air and sent a shiver of excitement up Rosie's spine.

She reveled in the exhilaration of the run, her complicated thoughts and emotions erased by the primal instincts that took hold. The pack caught the scent of a large buck shortly after they headed into the forest. Simon instructed them to surround him silently as he stalked forward, low to the ground. He lunged at the deer, and the chase was on. They kept pace with him, taking turns tearing large bits of flesh from his legs and body until he finally succumbed to his injuries and crashed to the ground. The deer let out a groan, and Simon jumped on him, sinking his teeth into its jugular, ending his suffering.

Normally they would run back to the house and change, coming back with the equipment to bring the deer back to the house for processing, but on a night like tonight, they feasted on the raw deer flesh under the moonlight.

After they ate, they ran. Simon led the pack through the forest, toward the ravine. A river cut through the bottom, and the soothing sound of the rushing water got louder and louder as they grew closer. When they reached the edge of the steep incline, they howled some more, letting their cries echo off the rocks below.

The pack started moving again, and Rosie followed Lucas closely. They ran along the edge of the ravine, the loud whoosh of the water below drowning out the sounds of the forest. Her attention zeroed in on her mate. The markings that ran along his back and down his legs were imprinted upon her memory. Mostly white along the front, he had a few brown markings along his snout and up his face, and his fur darkened to black along his back.

She slowed, suddenly realizing she couldn't feel the rest of the pack. Lucas turned away from the ravine and ran into a small clearing, where the moon cast a glow over the wildflowers and tall grass. She followed him, and he turned and rubbed his body against hers, nudging her gently. When his nose nuzzled the fur by her neck, it occurred to her that he'd purposely led her away. She nuzzled him back, enjoying the closeness.

"We'll get into trouble for getting separated from the pack," she said softly.

"I won't tell if you don't," he teased. *"Gossip will reach your dad by tomorrow morning. This might be our last chance to be alone for a while."*

"What will we tell him?"

"That we danced. There's nothing wrong with dancing."

Rosie nuzzled into his chest again. *"He'll be watching us closely."*

In the distance, Simon's long, low howl sounded.

"I think he's noticed we're gone," Rosie said. She felt mildly worried about her father's wrath, but it was worth it to feel so close to Lucas. She nudged him gently and licked the top of his head.

Another howl sounded, and Rosie sighed. *"I guess we should head back."*

"Not yet," Lucas said. He nuzzled her again, licking her face. *"Just a few more minutes."*

Rosie rubbed her body against his. A warm hum of electric energy ran between them, and they basked in it as they enjoyed a few minutes of silent closeness.

Something in the air shifted, and Rosie lifted her head. The malevolent energy reached her a moment before she heard rustling in the trees. Before she could call out a warning, the crack of a gunshot split through the silence of the night, and Lucas cried out in pain.

Rosie screamed, her heart skipping a beat as she watched him fall to the ground. He quickly scrambled back to his feet, favoring his front right leg.

"I'm okay, Rosie! Run!" He bit her hindquarters, pushing her along before he took off at a lopsided run.

Rosie raised her head and let out a long, urgent howl, praying her father was near, and followed Lucas as he set a slow, clumsy pace. After a few moments, he stumbled, unable to ignore his injury.

"Go, Rosie! Run!" He nipped at her, urging her

forward, but she stopped as his body gave out, and he collapsed to the ground.

"I'm not leaving you!"

Lucas's eyes rolled back in his head, and he went limp. Her stomach dropped, and she nudged him. His limbs moved slightly, and he whimpered.

Leaves rustled, and branches crunched under heavy boots. The hunter was coming closer. She stood over Lucas, trying her best to shield his body. Her heart hammered as the footsteps approached. A scent hit her. Tobacco. Aftershave. A jolt of panic ran through her.

"Get up, Lucas!"

He lay still, and she whined as she pulled at him.

The hunter crashed through the brush, into the open, where she could see him. Her thundering heart almost beat right out of her chest as she stared into Mason Lewis's face.

"I got one!" Mason yelled. "I got one!"

Behind Mason, Paul Lewis jumped out of the brush, followed closely by another hunter. Orange beanie and a full beard—and though it was the middle of the night, he wore sunglasses. His hate soured the air. The man from the diner—Beanie Man.

"We're too close to the Harts' house, Paul," Beanie Man said gruffly. "I hear voices. You'd better get your boy out of here!"

Relief flooded through Rosie, but the relief was short-lived when her ears didn't pick up the sound of voices. No other humans were coming.

Beanie Man was lying.

"But the red wolf!" Mason raised his gun toward Rosie.

"Go, Mason!" Paul scolded him. "I don't want

you caught out here. Take your truck, and get out of here."

"What about you?"

"Listen to your dad, son," Beanie Man said as he trained his gun on Rosie. "We'll load up the other truck with the kills and be right behind you."

Rosie crouched and growled as Mason ran off through the woods. The hunter's gun was trained on her, and she froze, trying to decide whether to stay and shield Lucas or charge forward and attack the hunter head-on. In the few seconds she took to weigh her options, the hunter suddenly fell forward as he was attacked from behind. Simon's large wolf form tumbled to the ground on top of the man then rolled off to the side. They were each down for only a moment before they both jumped to their feet.

"*Run, Rosie!*" her father shouted.

Her body flinched at her father's command, but the desire to protect Lucas overpowered her need to follow her alpha's orders. Rosie hunched over Lucas, covering his body, as her father faced off with Beanie Man. Paul raised his gun.

"*No!*" She ran forward, tackling Paul to the ground. He somehow managed to keep a tight grip on his rifle, and as he spun onto his back, he aimed at Rosie's chest.

Rosie was tackled from behind as the gun went off, and the bullet pierced the earth where she'd stood only a moment before. She tumbled to the ground in a tangle of limbs with her father. He leaped to his feet and bared his teeth.

"*Rosie, run!*" Simon's voice in her head lost its powerful tenor. He sounded desperate. Scared.

The next few moments were a blur. Her father tackled Paul and sank his teeth into his chest just as the crack of gunfire erupted and a spray of red hit Rosie's face. Rosie ducked to the ground before everything went silent.

Slowly, Paul maneuvered from under her father, and Simon's large mass of fur rolled limply to the ground in front of her. Her father's eyes stared sightlessly to the sky.

A scream ripped through Rosie's chest, but it came out as a strangled whine. *No. No, no, no, no.* Her brain fought against what her eyes were seeing. It couldn't be true. It couldn't be true. Time stood still, and the air grew thick. His eyes. His vacant eyes.

"Daddy?"

Rosie heard the cock of a gun and looked up to see Beanie Man pointing his rifle at her head. Survival instinct kicked in, and she turned to run, sprinting through the grass and past a small crop of trees—right to the rocky edge of the ravine.

Water rushed below, and she slid to a stop and peered down the steep incline. She turned just in time to see Beanie Man coming toward her, his rifle again aimed at her head, his finger on the trigger. He had her pinned. She closed her eyes, waiting.

Her eyes snapped open as she heard the cock of the gun. Instead of a gunshot, the gun made a strange click when he pulled the trigger. His body flinched, and he examined the gun angrily for a moment before he threw it into the grass and charged forward. She reflexively scrambled backward, and her stomach jumped to her throat as she plummeted over the edge of the ravine.

THIRTY-EIGHT

SAM

Sam kept his ears alert for anything out of
the ordinary, but it was nearly impossible in the forest. Strange sounds echoed off the trees. How Rosie
and Lucas had gotten separated from them was un-
clear. The pack had been running in a single-file line
when Michael had noticed the two youngest members were missing. Simon had called out to them with
a howl, but they hadn't heard a response.

Hoping maybe they had headed back to the
house, Simon sent Stuart and Roger there to look for
them. The rest of them spread out to search the
woods. Simon sent Sam and Michael to run along the
edge of the ravine just in case.

Sam told himself they would have heard Lucas
and Rosie if they'd fallen.

"I'm sure they're fine," Michael said. *"They probably just wandered off in the wrong direction."*

When they reached the ravine, Sam peered over
the edge. He tried not to think about them falling
down the steep incline filled with sharp, busted-up
tree roots and rocky outcroppings.

As they jogged along the edge, the sound of a gunshot echoed through the night, followed moments later by an urgent howl. Rosie was calling for help.

He took off at a run toward the sound of her cry, Michael hot on his heels. Sam jumped over tree roots and ducked through brush as fast as he could, praying for another howl from her to help him pinpoint her location.

He was so busy listening, he almost collided with Amos as he dashed in front of Sam from the opposite direction, followed closely by Daniel.

"Where's Dad?" Sam asked urgently, wanting to keep moving in Rosie's direction.

"He took off running when we heard Rosie's howl," Daniel said. *"We got separated when Amos tripped me."*

"I didn't trip you, you idiot," Amos said, seething. *"You were running in the wrong direction, and I ran into you."*

"What do you mean, I was 'running in the wrong direction'?" Daniel growled. *"I was following Simon!"*

"Enough!" Sam yelled. He began sniffing at the ground and the air, trying to catch the scent of any of their missing pack members.

The sound of another gunshot filled the air, and wordlessly, they all took off in the direction it had come from. Sam's stomach clenched. He tried not to let his mind run through gruesome scenarios before they knew what was going on, but the crack of yet another gunshot did nothing to ease his fears.

They zigzagged through trees and kept close to the ravine. Michael and Amos went off in one direction, and Sam and Daniel went in another.

Sam finally picked up Lucas's scent—intermingled with the strong smell of blood—and hurried his pace. They made their way along the edge of the ravine, and he heard the distinct sound of whimpering and short, mournful howls. It was then that he finally saw Lucas. His friend was lying at the edge of a cliff, his head hung over the side.

"*Lucas!*" Sam bolted toward him and sniffed, checking him for injuries. He was bleeding from his shoulder, and Sam licked at it, trying to assess the damage. It seemed like the bleeding was slow, and he didn't sense the injury was severe. Sam nudged him to try to get his attention. "*Where is Rosie? Where is my father?*"

Lucas didn't stop staring over the edge, continuing his low, mournful howls. Sam's stomach twisted as he followed Lucas's gaze down the side of the ravine. When he saw her, Sam almost stumbled over the edge. Rosie lay motionless at the bottom, her red hair splayed around her head, her pale skin glowing in the moonlight.

No.

Sam scrambled around the edge, trying to find some stable footing where he could make his way down. There had to be a way to get down there. He denied the reasonable part of his brain that told him there was no way she had survived that fall. He found a broken tree trunk a few feet below the edge, and he started to try to make his way toward it. She was okay. She had to be okay.

"*Sam! No!*" Daniel's voice cut through Sam's frantic thoughts as he bit at his tail. "*We'll have to go the long way around to get down there. It's too steep.*"

Sam was about to argue when they heard long howls of mourning a few dozen yards away.

"Dad," Sam whispered as he took off at a run toward them.

Seconds later, Sam found Michael and Amos standing over his father's human body. It was clear as he approached that his father was gone. Simon's lifeless eyes stared up at the sky.

"No!" he shouted. *"No!"*

Sam rushed to his father's side and sniffed him. The scent of blood and gunpowder assaulted his nose, making his stomach burn with anger and grief.

Rosie and their father. They were both gone. Anguish ripped through Sam's chest, and he raised his head toward the full moon and cried out a long howl, mourning the loss of his family.

THE REMAINING members of the pack went back to the house to change into human form and get the equipment they would need to retrieve the bodies of Rosie and Simon. Sam got dressed and picked up Rosie's and his father's clothes from the patio. They would need to dress them before they called the authorities. There would be questions when they arrived. Why they were out in the woods. Why Sam's father had a gunshot wound in his heart. Why Lucas had a gunshot wound in his shoulder.

Lucas waited at the ravine. He couldn't make the trek back on his own. Roger had been a wreck when they arrived at the house and told him what happened. He was worried for his son and wanted to get back to him as quickly as possible.

Michael remained silent as he hooked trailers up to the two ATVs in the garage. He pulled some blankets and tarps from the storage chest and put them into the trailers. Sam tried not to think about why they needed them. Michael climbed onto one of the ATVs and started the engine. Sam climbed onto the trailer behind it as Amos started the other ATV, and Roger sat in the trailer. Daniel stayed at the house with Stuart.

Sam's body jerked and jostled about as the ATV trailer hit bumps and tree branches on the forest floor, but he was numb to it. This didn't seem real. He couldn't think about his life without Rosie. She had been following him around since she could walk. She annoyed the hell out of him when she was little, but he would never tell anyone how much he loved the way she worshipped the ground he walked on. Rosie was the life in their house. She was their heartbeat. And the one person Sam would look to for guidance at a time like this was his father. He couldn't comprehend that he was gone.

Amos and Roger went to the top of the ravine to collect Lucas and Simon. Michael and Sam went to the east, where the ravine was less steep, and they made their way down to the riverbed and back up the bank to Rosie. They could only take the ATV part of the way there. The terrain was too rocky.

Sam picked up Rosie's clothes and a blanket and swallowed the lump in his throat as they started climbing over the rocks toward her. He never believed in prayer, but he said a silent one, wishing to the core of his being that they were on a rescue mission and not one of recovery. Rosie couldn't be gone—she just couldn't be.

When they spotted her, Sam's hand flew to his chest, and he stopped for a few moments to collect himself. Michael put a hand on Sam's shoulder, and they moved forward. As they approached, Sam saw blood marring the side of Rosie's face, where she had cracked her skull against the rocks. Her limbs were twisted and broken, lying at awkward angles. He prayed that she had been knocked out before her body was broken and that she'd felt no pain.

A hiccupped sob made Sam look at Michael. His cousin's eyes were red, and he held his fist to his mouth, fighting back another sob.

Sam stepped forward and knelt next to Rosie. Her face was always pale, but it was especially pale tonight, and it made her freckles stand out. Bruising circled her eyes, and as Sam looked over her body, he saw that she had more bruises along her arms and legs as well. He dared to let a tiny ray of hope light in his chest as he remembered learning in biology that the body didn't bruise after it was dead. He reached a shaking hand out and pressed it against her delicate wrist.

Th-Thump.

He couldn't believe it.

Th-Thump.

He left his fingers there a few moments longer just to be sure.

Th-Thump.

Th-Thump.

"Michael!" Sam screeched. "She's alive!"

The Hanks Hollow Series Continues...
Moon Over Hanks Hollow
Lost in Hanks Hollow
When Witches Wake

Dear Reader,

THANK YOU for reading *Witch in a Wolf Den*! These characters have become such a big part of my world, and I really hope you enjoyed meeting them. If you liked the story, please consider leaving a review on <u>Amazon</u> or <u>Goodreads</u>. Reviews and ratings help me so much, and I would be so grateful for the support!

For updates, follow me on Facebook, TikTok, or Instagram, and be sure to sign up for my newsletter!

https://linktr.ee/rachellekampen
https://www.facebook.com/rachellekampen
https://www.tiktok.com/@rachellekampen
https://www.instagram.com/rachellekampen/

ABOUT THE AUTHOR

Rachelle Kampen grew up on a farm in southern Wisconsin with three brothers and two sisters. In a rural setting with no cable television or internet, options for things to do were limited, so she read—a lot.

Though she's been writing stories from the time she learned to pen a sentence, she didn't take the leap into publishing until she started writing the Hanks Hollow series. The beloved characters and unique world of Hanks Hollow unite some of Wisconsin's fun quirks with a magical paranormal adventure.

She lives outside Madison, Wisconsin with her husband, daughter, two dogs, and two cats. Even now, with cable and internet at her fingertips, she loves a good book to pass the time.

You can find author Rachelle Kampen at:
https://linktr.ee/rachellekampen
https://www.facebook.com/rachellekampen
https://www.tiktok.com/@rachellekampen
https://www.instagram.com/rachellekampen/